## A Letter to Mama

Sawyer own me and Lulu? I cry. I never knew it!

Mark wrap each loaf in paper and tie it with string. You only five when it happen, he splain. Lulu but two. Both of you too yung to understand.

It don't make sense, I say. Sister and I, we live here in Gran's cabin. I am a free boy!

Sawyer is letting me raise you and Lulu, Gran reply, but he ain't signed your free papers yet. You still belong to him.

Then why don't Sawyer's wife know that? I ask. Why don't he tell her?

Gran lift her apron, dab a dot of sweat from her lip. Mark tell me that is enuf questshuns and leave her alone.

Mama, you need to come and get me. I don't want to belong to anybody but you.

## ALSO BY MARY E. LYONS

---

ROY MAKES A CAR

FEED THE CHILDREN FIRST:
IRISH MEMORIES OF THE GREAT HUNGER

DEAR ELLEN BEE:
A SCRAPBOOK OF THE CIVIL WAR

LETTERS FROM A SLAVE GIRL:
THE STORY OF HARRIET JACOBS

SORROW'S KITCHEN:
THE LIFE AND FOLKLORE OF
ZORA NEALE HURSTON

---

# Letters *from a* Slave Boy

The Story of Joseph Jacobs



Mary E. Lyons

Simon Pulse
New York London Toronto Sydney

This book is a work of fiction. Any references to historical events, real people, or real locales are used fictitiously. Other names, characters, places, and incidents are the product of the author's imagination, and any resemblance to actual events or locales or persons, living or dead, is entirely coincidental.

SIMON PULSE
An imprint of Simon & Schuster Children's Publishing Division
1230 Avenue of the Americas, New York, NY 10020

Also available in an Atheneum Books for Young Readers
hardcover edition.
Designed by Krista Vossen
The text of this book was set in Aldine.
Manufactured in the United States of America
First Simon Pulse edition January 2008
2 4 6 8 10 9 7 5 3 1
The Library of Congress has cataloged the hardcover edition as follows:
Lyons, Mary E.
Letters from a slave boy : the story of Joseph Jacobs / Mary E. Lyons.—1st ed.
p. cm.
Summary: A fictionalized look at the life of Joseph Jacobs, son of a slave, told
in the form of letters that he might have written during his life in
pre–Civil War North Carolina, on a whaling expedition, in New York,
New England, and finally in California during the Gold Rush.
ISBN-13: 978-0-689-87867-1 (hc)
ISBN-10: 0-689-87867-2 (hc)
1. Jacobs, Joseph, b. 1829—Juvenile fiction.
[1. Jacobs, Joseph, b. 1829—Fiction.
2. Slavery—Fiction. 3. African Americans—Fiction.
4. Letters—Fiction.]
I. Title
PZ7.L99556Let 2007
[Fic]—dc22
2006001277
ISBN-13: 978-0-689-87868-8 (pbk)
ISBN-10: 0-689-87868-0 (pbk)

*For Paul, for always*

# CONTENTS

# Cast of Characters

## Real

Joseph Jacobs's Family, Edenton, North Carolina

- Harriet: mother
- Gran (Molly): great-grandmother
- Samuel Sawyer: father, slaveholder
- Lulu (Louisa): sister
- John: uncle
- Mark: great-uncle
- Joseph: great-uncle

Other People in Edenton

- Dr. James Norcom: slaveholder
- Matilda Norcom: Norcom's daughter
- Josiah Collins III: slaveholder
- Josiah Collins IV: son of Josiah Collins III
- Wellington: enslaved coachman for Collins family

Boston, Massachusetts

- Frederick Douglass: abolitionist
- Abner Forbes: teacher
- William Simmonds: printer
- Thomas Sims: runaway slave

New York, New York

- Cornelia Grinnell: Harriet's employer
- James Tredwell: Samuel Sawyer's cousin
- Mary Tredwell: James Tredwell's wife
- Mr. Blount: Mary Tredwell's brother

New Bedford, Massachusetts

Moses Shepherd: owns boardinghouse

David Chase: ship's agent

William Grinnell: Cornelia Grinnell's father

Rodney French: abolitionist

Thomas Johnson: free sailor

California

John Sutter: owns mill where gold was first found

Runaway slave: taken captive after beating slaveholder

## Fictional

Old Dave Blount: banjo player

Comfort: enslaved girl

Apprentices: boys in print shop

Ivy Ann: whaling ship

Crew and officers of Ivy Ann

Negro Shallows: mining camp

Chinese tradesmen: run tent store in Mormon Island

Gold miners and poker players

Mulka: Nisenan Indian girl

## *Picture This . . .*

The year is 1830. The place is Edenton, a waterfront town in North Carolina. You're sixteen years old and the enslaved servant of Matilda Norcom, a seven-year-old girl. Your young brother, John, is a slave too. He's an office boy for Matilda's father, Dr. James Norcom.

The doctor is fifty-three years old and addicted to morphine. A violent man, he's the master of the Norcom household. Though you're his daughter's property, *he* holds the power over you.

The doctor learns that you'll soon be a mother. When you won't tell him who the father is, he throws you out of his house. You move in with your grandmother and her son, Mark. About six months later, you give premature birth to a boy whom you name Joseph.

Thankfully, your grandmother—white people in town call her Yellow Molly—is a free woman and owns her own cottage. She can support you and your infant by selling bread that she bakes in her kitchen. Living with her is a great comfort.

But the doctor refuses to let Molly buy your freedom, and he never lets you forget that you're still a slave. Molly's cottage is just down the street from his office and only two blocks from his town house. On his way to work, he often stops in to threaten you. One time he pitches you down the stairs. The bruises are so painful that you can't turn in bed for days.

Two years later Norcom finds out that you're expecting

another child. Furious, he comes to Molly's cottage and cuts your hair close to your head. When your daughter, Lulu, is born, he visits again and taunts you until you faint.

Despite Norcom's abuse, Lulu's sweet face and Joseph's childish giggles bring you much joy. It's a joy that could quickly turn to tragedy. According to law, the children are the property of Matilda Norcom. The law is brutally clear about this: the child follows the condition of the mother from the instant it is born. Legally, Joseph and Lulu are Matilda's slaves, just as you are. They can be sold at any time.

You never tell the children about their white father, Samuel Sawyer. In public, he doesn't claim them as his offspring. He seldom even sees them, since they aren't his slaves. You follow his wishes for privacy, because he's promised to purchase all of you one day, then set you free. You hold that picture of freedom in your mind, and it gives you hope.

Two years pass. Joseph is five, Lulu is a toddler of two. Now you're faced with a terrible dilemma. Dr. Norcom has built a lonely cabin in the woods outside of town. He wants you to live there so he can control you at all times. If you refuse, the children will be torn from your arms. "Your boy shall be put to work," he warns, "and he shall soon be sold. Your girl shall be raised for the purpose of selling as well."

Joseph put to work! The child is small for his age and sickly. He'd never survive the harsh conditions of field labor. And you can't let Lulu be raised in the Norcom household. She's afraid of the doctor's wife, who calls her a white-faced brat.

Frantic, you consider ways out of this desperate situation. Maybe you should flee with Joseph and Lulu. But could their little legs run for hours through the woods? Perhaps you should escape with them by ship. But what if a slave catcher comes aboard? Could Joseph and Lulu sit perfectly still in a hiding spot? *No,* you think. *My babies are too young to risk it.*

Should you run away alone, leaving the children with Molly? She could send them to you later—if you survive the escape. If you don't, they'll never see their mother again.

Or you could hide somewhere in Edenton. After all, Dr. Norcom is using the children to blackmail you. If he thinks you've escaped to the North, he might agree to sell them to Samuel Sawyer. Of the four possibilities, this one is the most dangerous. Edenton is a small town, so Norcom could easily find you. Captured runaways here are severely punished, even beheaded.

Which will it be? What decision will you make?

In June of 1835, an enslaved mother named Harriet Jacobs faced these same impossible choices. She chose the last one: She ran from Norcom and hid in Edenton to be near her children. Her first hiding spot was an upstairs room in a house owned by a sympathetic white woman.

Norcom was enraged. He organized patrols to search for Harriet and stationed night sentries through town. The next day he posted announcements that offered a one-hundred-fifty-dollar reward for her capture in North Carolina. Anyone who found her out of state would receive three hundred dollars. For the next eight weeks, he ran newspaper advertisements describing his "light mulatto" runaway. The ads stated that Harriet was probably headed north. Her ploy had worked; Norcom had no idea she was still in Edenton.

Soon after, Samuel Sawyer kept part of his promise to Harriet. He tricked the doctor into selling Joseph and Lulu to a slave trader. Then Sawyer bought them himself for five hundred dollars. He also paid nine hundred dollars for Harriet's brother, John.

When Norcom discovered the trick, he threatened to kill Molly and Mark and to whip John nearly to death. Harriet, of course, rejoiced when she heard that Sawyer now owned her children. Joseph and Lulu still weren't free, but at least they were out of Norcom's control.

By then it was time to move to a safer hiding spot. Late that same summer, Harriet quietly slipped into an enclosed storeroom on Molly's back porch. In the corner was a cupboard with a trapdoor at the top. It led to the crawl space beneath the eaves of Molly's roof. Molly's son, Mark, lifted Harriet up into a space about the size of two coffins. Molly passed food through the trapdoor, whispered messages in the dark of night, and carried away the slop pot. It was the beginning of a long ordeal.

Joseph and Lulu didn't know that their mother was living just over their heads. They were too young to keep such a dangerous secret, so Molly told them she had left for New York. But Harriet could hear them playing on the piazza below. After she hand-drilled a one-inch-round hole in the house wall, she could even see them playing in the yard.

Two years later, Samuel Sawyer had yet to give her children their free papers. One night she saw him passing on the street. She slipped down from her hiding spot. "All I ask," she whispered through a shuttered window, "is that you will free my children."

Sawyer agreed, but he must have known that this would ruin his reputation as a gentleman. To free Joseph and Lulu, he would have to appear before a judge and sign their emancipation papers. His signature would be a public confession to everyone in Edenton that the children were his offspring. He never could bring himself to do it.

Meanwhile, Harriet prayed that he would. Still a Norcom family slave, still waiting for Sawyer to free her children, she endured the crawl space. Almost seven years passed. Broiling heat, freezing temperatures, and raging fevers were her only companions in that hellish spot.

In *Letters from a Slave Girl: The Story of Harriet Jacobs*, readers imagine Harriet's suffering through her eyes. *Letters from a Slave Boy* is a tandem tale told through Joseph's eyes. It begins in Edenton while his mother is in hiding, then follows his journeys through the wider world. It is the story of a hunted woman's son—a boy who struggles to free his family and himself, and to decide who he really is.*

* Quotations in "Picture This" are from Harriet Jacobs's 1861 narrative, *Incidents in the Life of a Slave Girl*. Jean Yellin, ed. Cambridge, Harvard University Press, 2000.

# *Part* I

## Edenton, North Carolina

1839–1843

# Mama

EDENTON, NORTH CAROLINA
*3 April 1839*

Dear Mama,

As you can see, I no how to rite. A skinny stick of a white boy, name of Josiah Collins, is teeching me. He say, Joseph, rite down wurds that mean something to you. You will learn spelling soon enuf.

I meet Josiah this time last spring, round tree-leafing time. We standing on the fishing bridge, me at one end, him at the other.

He call out, Hey! How come you catch three stripey bass, while I only caught one?

Use short little fish for bait, I tell him. Then I give him baby shad from my bucket, and he catch two bass.

Next time I go to the bridge, Josiah show up with a pensul and old ledjer book. He rite alfabet letters in it to get me started. From then on, he been showing me how to turn letters into words and how to make punctuashun. He say it is a trade. I teech him to fish, he teech me to write.

Mama, I figure one fello in this family shood get some lerning. Your brother John can not read, leastways not before he run away from Mister Samuel Sawyer lass year. Great Uncle Mark can not ethur.

A boy is got to have his private thorts sometime. That is why Gran do not know bout this practice book. Only you, Mama, and it is our secrut.

Your good boy,
Joseph

---

*12 May 1839*

Dear Mama,

Lass nite I ask Gran again where you gone. She creak to her feet, poke at the coals in her bake oven.

Look in the sky, she say like always. Find the handle of the dipper. Your mama is working her way along that line of stars. They point to New York. To freedum.

And duz she miss me, I ask.

Same as if her right hand cut off, Gran reply.

And my daddy, where he, I ask again.

Stop pestering me, Gran order, or I will send a witch hag after you. Now go fetch a log.

Gran always say this when she want me to shut up. So I stomp outside to the woodshed. Stare up at the Big Dipper and look tord New York. The stars blink back, like they is smiling at such foolishness. I think them stars must be right.

I am nine years of age. That is too old to believe my mama is traveling thru the sky. And too old to believe the ghostie stories Gran tell. They is no such thing as hags, is they, Mama? Or plat-eye monsters?

Your son,
Joseph

---

*3 July 1839*

Dear Mama,

Something happen today that burn my bottom. I am walking down Broad Street, going to buy cinmun for Gran. Mister Samuel Sawyer pass by with his wife.

She call to me, What a pretty little negro! Who do you belong to?

I run home fast, tell Gran and Uncle Mark. Say I am a colored boy and do not like a white lady calling me negro. Or little, ethur. I am three and one half feet tall and growing every day.

Gran take her loafs of bread from the oven, slide in a pan of krackers. What folks call you don't matter, she say. It's what you answer to that matters.

But Gran, I ask, what the lady mean, who do I belong to?

A secrut look pass between Gran and Mark. The look that growed-up people think children don't see.

Joseph, she reply, remember when you was a teensy thing, and we have a big party? How we shut the curtains and light the candles?

I try hard, Mama, but nothing come to my mind.

The night we clap and sing, Mark remind me.

Oh, I say, when Lulu and I spin round the room, make ourselfs dizzy?

That's right, say Gran. That night we celebrate. Cause Sawyer buy you and your sister from Norcom, the man your mama run from.

Sawyer own me and Lulu? I cry. I never knew it!

Mark wrap each loaf in paper and tie it with string. You only five when it happen, he splain. Lulu but two. Both of you too yung to understand.

It don't make sense, I say. Sister and I, we live here in Gran's cabin. I am a free boy!

Sawyer is letting me raise you and Lulu, Gran reply, but he ain't signed your free papers yet. You still belong to him.

Then why don't Sawyer's wife know that? I ask. Why don't he tell her?

Gran lift her apron, dab a dot of sweat from her lip. Mark tell me that is enuf questshuns and leave her alone.

Mama, you need to come get me. I do not want to belong to anybody but you.

Your son,
Joseph

---

*29 August 1839*

Dear Mama,

They is bad news in this house today. I meet Josiah on the fishing bridge. When I get back, Gran is sniffling in her rocker. She say a free colored sailur stop by. He work the packet ship between Edenton and Boston, bring a letter from Uncle John. Uncle write that he is going off on a whaling trip.

Whales is giant sea monsters! Gran cry. One might swallow John whole, just like Jonah in the Bible.

But Gran, I ask, didn't that whale sick up Jonah after three days and nights? And didn't Jonah come out whole?

She smile a little, wipe her eyes. Yes, she answer, after Jonah pologize to God first. Your Uncle John is quick-tempered all right, but he always been slow to say he sorry.

I almost ask Gran what take Jonah so long. Been me, I'd a pologized right off. Not sit in a dark whale belly for three days first.

And I almost ask how come she know what the letter say. Gran can not read. Did the sailur read it to her? But two questshuns at a time is enuf for Gran, specially when she been crying.

Joseph

---

*December 1839*

Dear Mama,

More bad news. This morning I am helping Gran iron her best white tablecloths. She tell me that next year, Mister Sawyer might send Lulu to a place call Brooklyn, New York. She be under the care of his cuzin, James Tredwell, and his wife, Mary.

New York! That mean Lulu get to be with you, Mama!

I ask Gran, so Lulu seeing Mama?

Not zactly, Gran answer. Harriet might not be in New York just yet.

But Gran, I cry, Sister be living with strangers! Don't Sawyer know that her eyes get bad sometimes?

Lulu will be safer, say Gran, tho I wish he'd go on and give her the free papers. That slab of worry been hanging heavy over my head.

What he waiting for? I ask. I wrap a rag around my hand, pull an iron from the bake oven.

Gran spit on the iron, see if it hot enough. Say, I guess Sawyer don't want . . .

She stop herself, roll on to another subject.

Free papers is only half the problem, she say. Yesterday Dr. Norcom tell Sawyer you both still belong to his daughter. That she not of age when he sell you in her name. He brag that you and Lulu is still in his power.

Gran lay one end of the cloth on the table. I hold up the other end, wonder what she talking bout. She slap the iron down like she squashing bugs. Iron go *slap, slap!*

Norcom might take his claim to a judge, she say. If the judge rule the sale been illegal, you and Lulu belong to Norcom's daughter again.

*Slap!* go that iron. Then Norcom might send you out to his plantashun. Make you cut cornstalks from sun to sun.

Let him try! I holler, dropping the cloth. I will whack him down!

Joseph, Gran reply, we got to bide our time. Unball your fists and leave well enough alone.

But Mama, I hear that Norcom's overseer ride the fields with a horsehair whip in his meaty hands. He beat any slave who beg for water or try to rest a while. You know what's the truth? I am skeered.

Joseph

---

*1 June 1840*

Dear Mama,

We wait all winter for Norcom to see the judge, try to take me and Lulu back. Gran say he put her in mind of a cottonmouth snake. Hiding in the shallows, waiting to slide up and bite.

And now I got me a new worry. Today I am standing at the street end of Gran's cabin. I hear a raspy noise coming from over the woodshed. Sound like your cough, Mama. That cannot be true, I tell myself. Cause you is far from here, heading north.

Then I wonder if I am hearing a plat eye. Maybe it is taken the shape of a hunchback hog. Maybe it is in the shed, rooting around for the flesh of a boy!

I do not speak of the noise to Gran. I do not want

her thinking she can still scare me with them shape changer stories.

Or Josiah, ethur. In the winter, he at his daddy's Somerset plantashun across the sound. But it is too buzzy with skeeters over there now. His family spend some of the hot months at their town house here on Edenton Bay.

Josiah a lucky boy. He got two houses. And he get to see his mama every day.

Joseph

---

*15 July 1840*

Dear Mama,

Lass night I dream a five-legged cow is running me down. It is a plat eye, with boiling yellow eyes and a long ruff tongue. Just when it catch up, I hear whispering.

Go to sleep, it say, and remember never to tell. I wake up a little, think, that ain't no plat eye. That is Gran talking to Lulu! Then I wonder if Gran and Lulu is turn into hags during the night. Been flying over the moon on straw brooms.

I make up my mind to ask Lulu about it in the

morning. But Sister leave too quick. At dawn, Sawyer's carriage come to Gran's cabin. It is carrying him, his wife, their baby, and the baby's nurse.

Mama, it been a sad thing, watching Mark lift Lulu through the carriage door. She only eight years old. Will that cuzin in New York wipe her eyes when they get red and swollen?

And it make me mad to rite the name of Samuel Sawyer. So what if he a rich congressman? Or got fifty slaves waiting on him at his town house, and lots more on his plantashun? That do not give him the rite to send Sister away to a strange place without free papers.

I will miss Lulu. Miss her chasing me through the woods, calling, Brother, wait up! and her muslin dress astreaming round her legs. Now, you know a boy don't want his little sister going fishing with him. But the truth is, I am sorry I did not let her come along. Not every time, a course, but at least once or twice.

Your son,
Joseph

*9 October 1840*

Dear Mama,

After the noon meal today, Gran say, Joseph, you ten years old. Big enough to feed the animals, carry the wood, *and* do your sister's chores.

Double chores, Mama! It ain't fair. Well, I slop the hogs like Lulu used to. But I only sweep the front piazza, not the yard. Then I go upstairs and pull my ledjer from under the bed. Practice riting till Gran come plowing after me. When she see the book, she say, what on erth?

Josiah Collins give it to me, I say. He teeching me to rite.

Gran sit on the bed, pluck at the covers. Time you learn the story, Joseph, she say real slow. My youngest son name Joseph too. Your mama name you after him. He a bold boy, too daring for a slave.

Your Josiah's daddy is Josiah Collins the third, she go on. He own my Joseph and whip him one time. My boy run away, get as far as New York. An Edenton white man spot him, send him back here. Collins chain my pet, lock him in the Edenton jail.

I tell Gran, stop, cause it look like she ready to fall out. But she stumble on through the story, make me listen.

Three months later, Gran say, Collins the third sell Joseph to a slave trader going to New Orleans. Joseph escape again, and I get word he is leave the country forever. Say he won't be treated like a dog.

Then Gran order me, stay away from that Collins boy. You see him again, plat eye going to get you!

Aw, Gran, I say. Josiah will not hurt me. He can not even catch a fish unless I help him.

Gran do not answer and go back downstairs. Now her rocker legs is beating against the floor. I know that sound. It mean she is sewing to calm herself. Punching a needle through a tablecloth hem like she boxing with it.

Mama, I can not help it if Josiah decide to meet me on the bridge. Besides, he somebody to laff with. That mean a lot, cause there ain't been a hangnail's worth of fun round here since Lulu left. I am terrible sick of worrying about her eyes and wondering if a judge will give us back to Norcom one day.

Anyway, Josiah don't treat me like a slave. He never would.

Joseph

*June 1841*

Dear Mama,

Here is what has happen since last I wrote.

Near as Gran can tell, Norcom is not spoke to a judge yet.

Samuel Sawyer still holding out on my free papers.

I am now eleven years of age and four feet tall.

They is been no more sign of plat eyes or hags in this house.

Gran don't know I still meet Josiah on the fishing bridge.

Josiah think my spelling improve over the winter. He been teeching me new marks. They look like rabbit ears, go round words people say.

I been to two sociables at Hayes Plantation. One at planting time in April, and one last month when the shad start running. Old Dave Blount at both. He live in the quarter at Hayes. That fella can pluck a gourd banjar like he got four hands.

And what do you think of this? A girl name of Comfort belong to Mr. Hayes. She live in the quarter too, so I see her at both frolics. One minute she grinning at me. Next minute she calling me names like runt and hog bottom.

I tell Josiah about Comfort. He say, "Joseph, she must be sweet on you."

"Take it back," I holler, "or I will knock you silly, you chicken-chested sack of fish bones!"

Then Josiah tell me about a girl name of Sallie. She and her family visit Somerset for days at a time. When they have tea, Josiah has to play host. But he hate holding those little bitty cups, and Sallie never open her mouth. She just perch on a chair, giggle the whole time.

Josiah and I, we do not know what girls think is so funny.

Your son,
Joseph

---

*July 1841*

Dear Mama,

Bass leaping high this week, like they can't wait to sizzle in Gran's fry pan. This afternoon I walk over to the head of Queen Ann's Crick to catch me a few. Pretty soon Josiah come along with a poplar pole.

He say his family going north, and he want to teach me some new words before he leave. After he write them in the mud, I trace them three times with my fingers. I teach him something back. Tell him not to use poplar for poles, cause it is weak wood and break too easy.

When the sweat start rolling, we strip our shirts, go wading. He put his bare arm next to mine. "Joseph," he say, "you're as white as I am!"

"Shoot," I answer, "you so white, you look blue!"

By late afternoon, the sun is turn us the color of tea. We name ourselves the Brown Joes, cause we got the same skin color, same brown curly hair, and almost the same name. Born in the same year, too. And both short but growing yet.

Mama, some white boys round here is streak with meanness. Act like even they poop is lily white. Josiah, he different.

Your son,
Brown Joe

---

*September 1841*

Dear Mama,

Brown Joe back from the north but leaving for Somerset tomorrow. Today we lie on the bank of the crick, wait for a bite. It feel good, being lazy as a cloud. I like how the trees across the way double themselves and turn upside down in the water.

"School is starting soon," Josiah says with a sigh, "if Papa can find a new tutor."

"What happen to the old one?" I ask.

"Our twenty-five dogs took care of him."

"You mean they eat him?" The thought give me a shiver.

Brown Joe laugh. "Naw, my little brothers and I let them have the run of the schoolhouse, just like they're people. The tutor couldn't stand the barking another second. He left Somerset back in the spring."

"Don't your daddy care that you boys give the teacher a bad time?"

"Oh, Papa is too busy giving supper parties and dances to keep up with us."

I ponder this some. "Brown Joe, I hear that a long time ago your daddy whip my great-uncle Joseph. Is it true?"

"Well, this is the first I've heard of it," Josiah says. "Our plantation has three hundred slaves. I don't know the particulars of each one. Anyway, it happened before I was born. It has nothing do with me."

Josiah tie bait on his line. "Joe," he say real solemn, "I am sorry about your great-uncle. But I would never hurt you or anyone in your family. I swear it."

Mama, I look for the truth in Josiah's eyes while he make that silvery promise. Then I think about Norcom going back on his bill of sale. And Sawyer never giving Lulu or me our free papers. Seem to me white people always say one thing, do the other.

Another chill ripple over my bones, and I pick up a stick. Ask Josiah to write "particulars" in the dirt so I can trace it with my finger. About that time, he get a bite, and there is no more talk of whippings.

Joe

# Lulu

*10 June 1842*

Dear Lulu,

It is terrible quiet around here. Only sound I hear is the whirr of a cricket and the tick of the mantel clock. Gran near done in with grief and worry. Eat a few bites of bean stew a while ago, then nod off in her rocker. Mark left to visit a free woman name of Ann that he got an eye for.

But I got to share the news with somebody. Gran say that Sawyer's cousin sposed to send you to school in Brooklyn, so maybe you can read these letters one day.

Lulu, Gran been telling me for years that Mama is following the stars to New York. You have hear her say it yourself. But as you know, it been a long deep lie. Cause today I find Mama and lose her again, all at the same time. It hurt bad, like a splinter in my toe, or a leg boil too red to touch.

Here is what happen. This afternoon I am standing by the house gate. The sky is so clean, I can see smoke rising from Hayes. With all my chores done, it look like a good time to get the pole.

Just then, Gran come outside. She whisper, "Go to the storeroom."

I step inside the back piazza and peek round the storeroom door. And who do I see but Mama, easing out of the corner cupboard, limp as yarn! Weren't for leaning on the flour barrel, she might of topple over.

And she is paler than dead fish in a bucket. This worry me, till she stretch out her arms. I go to her, and she give me a big squeeze. Then she seem like our mama again.

She tell me she is never left Edenton at all. That she been hiding under the roof all these years. When I remember the cough, it all make sense.

"Mama," I ask, "is you the one read Uncle John's letter to Gran?"

"Yes," she answer.

"And did Gran bring Lulu to you the night before Lulu leave?"

When Mama say yes again, Gran's whispering that night make sense too. So it were you two talking,

Sister, and not a plat eye or hag, after all, and I am mighty glad of it.

But I figure there is no need in Mama thinking she got a spooked cat for a son. "Mama," I lie, "one time I hear a cough, and I know it been you!"

She tear up, say, "Sometimes I could hear you, too, Joseph. But all that is behind us now. When the shadows fall, I am sailing away from this place, if Norcom do not spy me on the street."

Mama pull a nut from a chestnut tree out of her pocket, press it in my palm. "This buckeye for good luck, my little man. If you hold it tight, we will be together soon."

Around sunset, when it look like God is lit a candle behind the sky, I help Mama from her hole. We wait for the candle to go out. Then her friend Peter come and walk her to the dock.

Soon as she wave good-bye, I race round the corner to Norcom's house. Look in his parlor window and see him dozing in a chair. Back I go through the alleys, praying hard that Mama is not left yet. When I come out through the trees, I spot her with Mark at the edge of the dock. I catch up and tug on her arm.

"Don't worry," I whisper, "the doctor is home. He won't see you."

Mama run one finger down my cheek, and Mark help her into the dinghy. Then Peter row her toward a steamer ship sitting out in the bay. I watch till her face disappear, and all I can hear is the oars, creaking in the iron locks like they in pain.

When I get back home, I notice my fingers is froze up. Look down to see Mama's smooth brown nut held tight in my hand all that time.

I wonder, Lulu. Can a person squeeze all the luck out of a buckeye? Or maybe it is bad luck to give good luck away. Mama might need that buckeye herself real soon.

Joseph

---

*15 July 1842*

Dear Lulu,

Mama safe! We get a letter from her today, mail by the ship captain in Philadelphia. When it come, Gran settle in her rocker with a catfish grin on her face.

"Read it, Joseph," she tell me, and I do. Then she snatch it from my hand and quick throw it in the oven.

"Gran!" I holler.

"Hold on," she say. "What if Norcom walk in to buy some of Yellow Molly's crackers? He might spy your mama's handwriting on the envelope."

Mark agree, so Mama's letter is ashes now. But I remember the particulars. She going to settle herself in New York and get a job. When Gran got enough money for my ship ticket, I go to New York too!

"Sawyer *got* to sign the boy's free papers," Mark mutter. "Maybe I should talk to him. . . ."

Gran look doubtful, say, "Can't none of us make him do what ain't in his heart."

Then she say free papers or not, I be away from Norcom's clutches, and that is one more rung up the freedom ladder.

Joseph

---

*15 October 1842*

Dear Lulu,

How is things in Brooklyn? Is you seen Mama yet? Tell her a lot happening here in Edenton. Mark and Ann have decide they is marrying! Ann own a cabin, so they living there after the wedding.

Mark always seem old, Lulu. He never talk much, and his face got more lines than bark. Today, though, he look handsome. When I tell him so, he make a shy smile.

He say, "First time in forty-two years I be on my own."

"But you marrying Ann," I tease. "Then you belong to her."

He laugh. "And she belong to me. Taking care of each other, Joseph, that's what getting married is for. You promise to always put the other first. Then you keep your promise. A man who don't keep his promises is no man at all."

Then Mark tell me how a husband take care of a wife. But I cannot write it down, Lulu, cause you a girl and too young, besides.

Joseph

---

*17 October 1842*

Dear Lulu,

Corn-shucking party at Hayes tonight. Gran want me to stay home and try on a suit she sewing. Mark say, "Oh, let the boy go. He need a chance to grow up some before he go north."

Old Dave Blount at the party with his banjar. Comfort there too. After everybody eat, we all dance in the moonlight. She hold my hands real tight while we sashay down the line for the Virginia Reel.

After the reel over, she sidle up to me. "You a

fine dancer," she whisper. "Got a nice smile, too."

While Comfort talk, I miss every lick Dave hit on the banjar.

Girls take up too much time.

Joseph

---

*Christmas Eve 1842*

Dear Lulu,

Old Dave come to the house today. I am surprise to see him carrying a new gourd banjar. He make it just for me, and it is the prettiest thing I ever own. Got a groundhog-skin head, with one short catgut string and three long ones.

While Gran fix snowball cakes, Dave show me how to play. "Slide your left fingers down the strings," he tell me. "Pluck with your right."

When Dave play, rhythm go *plunk plunkity, plunk plunkity*. He call it knocking. When I try, rhythm go *plunk dah plunk dah plunk*.

I tell him, "Dave, my fingers is stiff as hooves!"

"Sound like it too," Gran put in.

Dave laugh. "You'll catch on," he say. "Just give it time."

After Dave leave, I ask Gran, "How much time *do* I have?"

She go to her trunk and pour a bag of coppers on the table. "Three or four months," she answer.

"Gran, Mark is soon moving into Ann's house. When I leave, you won't have nobody to help you."

"I be fine," she answer, but her voice crack like an eggshell.

"Come with me," I beg.

She put down her stirring rod, hold out her gnarly hands.

"See these? They seventy-three years old, but God keep life in them yet. The more I bake, the more I can save for when somebody need it. And ain't it cold as Norcom's soul up there in the North? My bones achy enough as it is."

"Then I won't go."

Gran pour the batter in the cook pot and sit beside me. "Lordy, Lordy," she sigh. "Your last years of childhood belong to your mama, not me."

I jump up, cry, "I ain't a child! I am thirteen. Nearly. Almost."

"Mm hm," Gran say. "Your birthday in April. That's four months off. But, all right then, if you such a man, go fix the roof over your mama's old hidey-hole. Mark patch it with carpet scraps last winter, but it still leaky. Go on, now. Climb up there and nail down a board."

Lulu, do you know how a grown-up win an argument? They give you a chore, think that is the end of it. By the time I figure out how to climb on the roof with a board, my Christmas mood is clear gone. I don't like being so high, either. While I wobble round, I puzzle over what to do.

Stay here to take care of Gran but break Mama's heart? Join Mama and leave Gran all alone? When I look down in Mama's hidey-hole, I wonder how she stand it so long. Then I remember she do it to be near you and me, and I see the answer clear.

Joseph

---

*25 December 1842*

Dear Lulu,

This Christmas Day start high as angels. Gran give me the new suit she been sewing. It is brown with black suspenders and a white tie. Make me look like a preacher. Then she serve a big Christmas feast on her best tablecloth. How we did eat, Sister! Stuffed turkey, hominy grits, roast quail and rice, turnip greens boiled with Irish taters, sweet potato pie.

After that, the day flatten down. I meet Brown Joe

at the water's edge in front of his daddy's house. Give him a strong hickory pole, show him how it bend without breaking. Then here come Wellington down the slope. He the coachman for the Collins family.

"Josiah," he say, "your papa want you."

Joe look like he been caught with his britches down. He cut his eyes away from me, slink toward the house. "Brown Joe!" I yell. "Where you going?"

"Don't call me that!" he yell back. "Father says you should address me as young master!" Then he run off.

Wellington put his big hand on my shoulder. "Last night Mr. Collins order Josiah not to see you anymore. Think it ain't right for a white boy of his station."

Lulu, I know Brown Joe like my own nose. When Gran tell me not to fish with him, I pay her no mind. Josiah will do the same. Come spring, he will be on that fishing bridge.

Joseph

---

*4 April 1843*

Dear Lulu,

Winter weather finally gone. Josiah is not whip me like his daddy whip our great-uncle Joseph. But they is other ways to hurt a person, hurt him bad. I been to the bridge a few times. Never do see Brown Joe.

So I give up fishing, having lost my taste for bass. Been thumping my banjar every spare minute, instead. Playing "Roustabout," a tune I learn from Old Dave.

That is why I am home when the free colored sailor from Boston arrive this afternoon. He bring a letter from Mama.

First thing she write is that Uncle John is back from his whaling trip and living in Boston. Gran's face light up like a lantern when I read that part.

"Sea monster can't swallow him now!" she whoop.

Second, she write that Norcom got spies and snoops all over New York City. But coloreds there got big ears too. A few weeks ago they give Mama a warning.

Norcom think he know where she living in New York, and he going there to catch her. So Mama leave the married couple she work for on Long Island. Go straight to Boston and hide at John's place.

"The snake still under the rock," Mark say. "I seen Norcom just this morning, walking to his office."

None of us say what we thinking. If the doctor do go north and find Mama, he can kidnap her, bring her back here. Some white masters make an example of a runaway. Lay the lash on they back, or lock they head in stocks on the courthouse green till they faint or die.

Gran lean back in her rocker, sigh deep. "He could

kill her if he want," she say after a time, "and still be within the law."

"By God," I cry, "I will stomp the man if he touch Mama!"

Gran bolt straight up, and her eyes fly open. "Joseph, leave God out of it. You mess with Norcom, he might take a notion to speak to that judge after all. Now, what else your mama write in that letter?"

"She want me to sail to New York right away," I tell her. "An Edenton man who run away from slavery is meeting me at the pier, taking me to see Lulu in Brooklyn. Then he putting me on a ship to a place call Connecticut. From there, I ride the train to the city of Boston."

Sister, you know what this mean? I be seeing you soon! And I am bringing all these letters, so you can read them at last.

Joseph

---

*10 April 1843*

Dear Lulu,

Today I walk over to the burying ground. Bow my head and say good-bye to Mama's daddy and mama and two aunts. Poor Gran. She is lose every daughter she have. The pine trees she plant by each grave is nearly as tall as me now. I clear away the dead brush round them, then head over to Hayes plantation.

Old Dave in the smokehouse, pulling down a ham. When I tell him I am leaving, he take me outside. Make me sit on a stump and play his banjar. He close his eyes and listen, say, "Your strum is good and limber now."

Dave start to show me me a new tuning, but Comfort come down the path toting a basket of laundry. He grin, tell me he got to go see a man bout a race horse.

"Don't leave yet," I beg, but Dave disappear then. Comfort drag me in the smokehouse, pucker up her lips. And that is all I got to say about that.

Joseph

---

*11 April 1843*

Dear Lulu,

Gran's clock ticking away. When the little hand lands on ten, I got to go. She is pack me a carpetbag with five shillings, three ham biscuits, two shirts, and an extra pair of trowsers. And she is made a quilted carrying bag for my banjar. Early this morning she go to the dock, buy my ticket. Come back clicking her tongue.

"Sometimes them steamships blow up," she mumble.

That is true, Lulu. I have heard tales of such from colored watermen down at the dock. They tell of passengers blowing sky-high, falling back down in bloody chunks.

Gran wrap a cord round the banjar bag, knot it tight enough to choke a chicken. "Anybody ask who you belong to, you tell them Samuel Sawyer."

"But what if I meet up with a slave ketcher on the ship? What if he don't believe a colored boy, and he haul me off when the ship dock?"

"What if is a big hole," say Mark. "Think about it too much, you might fall in."

"But, Mark, I feel like a possum! Animal run this way and that, till the dogs circle in. Before you know it, that possum is somebody's supper."

Mark look tore in two. "I'll go with him," he tell Gran.

"No!" I cry. "Bad enough with Mama leaving, then Lulu, now me. Who be left to take care of Gran?"

Mark sit me down, look me hard in the eye. "I won't lie to you, son. You *is* something like a trapped possum. No telling if or when Norcom might go to the judge. You still got no free papers. Slave ketchers and kidnappers is prowling the high seas and the low roads."

"They's laws against kidnapping," Gran say. "But laws don't mean much to a slavery-loving judge. That's why you got to think like a man now."

"A smart one," Mark add. "The captain says you can sleep below deck tonight. Till then, keep your head low and your mouth closed. Don't be sassing anybody."

"And one more thing," Gran put in. "Write letters if you want, but only in your ledger book. Don't mail any down here. They might put Norcom on the scent of your mama's trail. Anyway, without you, ain't nobody left in this house can read them."

Gran pull her shawl round her shoulders and sink in her rocker. Close her eyes and whisper the Lord's Prayer. I kneel down, take her hand.

"Gran," I promise, "we all be together again sometime." She nod but do not open her eyes or even say good-bye.

Mark getting ready to walk me to the wharf, Lulu. I got to stop, put this ledger in the carpetbag. Already put in Mama's lucky buckeye to keep the ship from blowing up. If it work, I be seeing you soon. If it don't, buckeyes ain't worth the trouble.

Your brother,<br>
Joseph

# Part II

## Boston, Massachusetts

1843–1846

# Gran

*11 April 1843*

Dear Gran,

I reckon old Norcom can't get me now, cause this ocean is a wide place. The sky is blue as chicory flowers, and the wind taste salty sweet, like taffy.

The sailors is friendly. Five is working the ship, two of them colored. One say, "Boy, you want to catch the best breeze? Stand on the foredeck, by the bulwarks."

I ask what that mean.

"Foredeck is the front of the ship," he answer. "Bulwarks is the sides."

Gran, if you see Josiah Collins on the street, you stop him where he stand. Tell him Joseph Jacobs is learning new words on his own.

Your great-grandson,
Joseph

*13 April 1843*

Dear Gran,

You never saw such goings on as in the city of New York. When the ship dock, Mama's friend walk me to Sawyer's cousin's house in Brooklyn. But it is not like walking at home. The buildings is scrunched up close as fingers on a hand, and folks buck along like they shoes on fire. I keep a lookout for Norcom's pointy head, but they is too many people to watch at once.

Mama's friend leave me at the steps of Mr. James Tredwell's house, say he be back in twenty minutes. Miz Mary Tredwell open the door and call for Sister like she a fetch-it slave.

"Lulu," she holler up the stairs, "come down here!"

I look around, see paint peeling from the walls. Miz Tredwell looking right shabby herself. Fuzzy cuffs, shoes run-down at the heel. What you call low folk, Gran.

She take me to the parlor and scuffle out. Then Lulu come in. Right off, I notice she got a sad face. Her eyes is red, and her dress thin-looking, like it been scrubbed too many times. We sit on the divan for a while, but she don't say nothing.

"Is the Tredwells working you too hard?" I ask.

Lulu stare at her hands, say, "A little. I am the waiting maid for their baby girl."

I pull the ledger from my carpet bag, think the letters might cheer her some.

"Look, Sister! I been writing you!"

But she shake her head. That's when I know the Tredwells has never send her to school.

"Why don't Mama come see me lately?" Lulu ask.

"Cause she run away to hide in Boston with Uncle John. I am taking a ship to Connecticut, then a train to Boston."

"Oh, Joseph," she cry, "I want to go too!"

Lulu put her fingers on her lips, then I follow her out to the yard. We squinch down behind the grapevine arbor while she tell me a secret.

"Mr. Tredwell drink too much," Lulu say. "And his wife got a brother name of Mr. Blount who drink with James. Sometimes they send me to the shops for more rum or brandy. If they hands shake, I got to pour it. When Mr. Blount drink too much, he speak wicked words in my ear."

Lulu lower her voice to a whisper. "They is not things a gentleman would say. And he got sour breath, bad as a mangy dog."

About then, Miz Tredwell call for Lulu to change the baby's clothes. "Promise not to tell Mama," Lulu beg.

"I swear it," I say. Then I give her Mama's buckeye

and a good-bye hug. I do not say I am scared for her. Look to me like Mister Tredwell is fallen on hard times. Lulu got no free papers. What's to keep him from taking her south, selling her to a slave trader? By the time Samuel Sawyer find out, it be too late. We might never see Sister again.

Your Joseph

---

*Seven p.m.*

Dear Gran,

I am on the ship to Connecticut. Things ain't going too good. Been sitting on a pile of rope, not talking to anybody, just like you say. Now the sun is gone, and the wind been cutting me up.

A little while ago, a gray-head old colored porter pass by. He got a pile of pillowcases and sheets in his arms. "Can you take me below deck?" I ask. "Show me where to sleep?"

"Look here," he answer. "The cabin is only for white folks, and these linens for their berths. You want a place out of the wind, go to the forecastle. Sleep in the passage by the boiler room."

Gran, I think the forecastle is down in the eye of the ship, and berth is another word for bed. But I do not know where the boiler room is, or what they boil in there.

Joseph

---

*14 April 1843*
*Eight a.m.*

Dear Gran,

This trip about ruint. The boiler room hot and fiery, like a little closet in hell. When I look inside, I see a white boy shoveling coals in a firebox. The coals make fire, the fire make steam, and the steam make the paddle wheels turn. I guess if the ship blow up, it start in the boiler room.

Well, I settle down in the passageway, like the man tell me. Take a shirt and the trowsers from the carpetbag, ball them up for a pillow. But light from the firebox tickle my eyelids, and the engine roar do not let up. I never do sleep, for thinking about a splosion.

Gran, you will not like this next part. I am so

sleepy this morning, I forget and leave the clothes by the boiler room. But they staying there, cause I am not going back to that bad-dream hole.

Bell ringing now. This mean the ship dock in half an hour. Then I ride the cars. I am praying that if any Southerners on the train, none of them be slave ketchers hunting for a colored boy to steal away.

Joseph

---

BOSTON
*15 April 1843*

Dear Gran,

They is a heap to tell you! First, Boston is a puzzle of a city. The streets is crookedy and narrow, some nearly as steep as a church roof. It is cold and windy, too. No wonder people shuffle along, they backs rounded in a half hunch. In Edenton the water be warming up by now. Here, they is a skin of ice on the harbor, and the trees still naked.

After the train pull into Providence Depot, I hop off, follow directions in Mama's letter. Run past the Common till I reach the North End. Mama write that this is where most colored newcomers in the city live.

I find Uncle John's boardinghouse and dash up the steps. When I reach the third floor, I pound on the door. Mama crack it an inch till she see my face, then she throw it open.

"Here I am, Mama!" I say. "I come alone and run all the way!"

She laugh and hug me till Uncle John step out of a little sleeping room. It been five years since I seen him, and he is so changed, you would hardly know him yourself, Gran.

Uncle got the same eyes that cut straight through you. Same dark caramel skin. But years on the whaler give him the shoulders of a bear and a slash of wrinkles on each cheek. While Mama unpack the carpetbag, he pump my hand.

"How is your sister?" John ask.

I almost say what's sitting top on my mind—that the Tredwells might sell Lulu. But I hold back, don't want nothing to chase Mama's smile away. I keep a clamp on Lulu's secret, too.

"Sister don't know so much as I do," I brag. "Cause I can read, and she can't." Then I tell how I lost my clothes coming.

"You arrived safely," Mama say. "That's all that matters."

I got to close now, Gran. The lady who run the boardinghouse is fixing codfish chowder. The thick steamy smell of it make me hungry. I think I like Boston.

Joseph

---

*6 April 1843*

Dear Gran,

Mama and Uncle John take me to a boy's clothing shop today. They buy me a warm coat, new shirt, and a cap. On the way, we see lots of folks on the street, all a different color. Remind me of nubs on an ear of corn—white, black, yellow, every shade of brown.

Not all the white folks is highborn. We pass a white family standing on the curb. They got six children thinner than string, each one holding out they little hands to me.

"Mama," I ask after we pass by, "how come white people here so poor?"

"The city is full of Irish," she reply, clipping every word. "More arrive every year."

"Famine strikes almost every year in Ireland," Uncle John add. "The people flee when they can."

"Well," I say, "I am glad I am not Irish."

Mama disagree. "I would ten thousand times

rather see my children as half-starved paupers of Ireland," she say, "than the most pampered slave in America."

I guess Mama right about the Irish. I never been half-starved, so I do not know.

Your Joseph

---

*17 April 1843*

Dear Gran,

The white lady Mama work for in Long Island has send welcome news. Norcom's spies *did* give him directions to her house. But when he knock on her door, she tell him Mama don't live there anymore. Now old prune lips is back in Edenton, and Mama gone back to Long Island.

So Mama is left me again, Gran. But I guess that is all right, cause she can check on Lulu in Brooklyn, see how she doing. Only thing is, I am mostly by my lonesome. Last night Uncle John stay out late at an antislavery meeting. He leave early this morning, go to his job at an apothecary shop.

I am wishing I could come home for a bit. Play a tune or two with old Dave, dance with Comfort a while. Boston full of people and buildings, but it feel empty as the sky today.

Joseph

*19 April 1843*

Dear Gran,

Last night John go to a lecture by an escape slave. His name Frederick Douglass. Uncle all in a bother when he get home—pacing the room, dark eyes flashing.

"Abolitionists will break the yoke of slavery!" he shout. "We shall seek liberty, if we have to travel through the gates of death!"

John's temper scare me some, so I change the subject, quieten him down. "Is whales really monsters, Uncle?"

John take a breath, settle in a chair. "Yes, compared to the size of a man, they are. Some are more than sixty feet long."

Sixty feet, Gran! At least Jonah had some fidget room while he down in that whale belly.

"Whaling is a rough life," John go on. "It's mostly blood and guts. The only good I got out of it was reading. I worked my way through a trunk of books. You would do well to read more yourself, Joseph."

"If whaling so bad, how come you go?"

"Many escaped slaves join whaling crews. I knew that Samuel Sawyer couldn't find me on the sea. And I needed the money, little as it was."

John pick up the oil lamp on the table. "My ship returned with over three thousand barrels of this whale oil. That meant a share of the profit for all hands aboard. I planned on using mine to pay someone to get your mother out of her hiding hole. When I discovered she was living in New York, I was a happy man."

I tell John I do not understand how a whaling ship can hold so much or go so far.

He say, "My ship weighed four hundred and seven tons. It was big enough to sail down around the tip of Africa. Then it headed into the Pacific Ocean, where whales run like shad."

"But Uncle, that sound like the best fishing trip in the world! Ain't it exciting to spear one of them giants?"

"Joseph, leave whaling alone. You've got better things to do with your life."

After that, John turn out the lamp, and we climb in bed. While he snore, I throw lances in my mind. I want to see the wide Pacific, Gran. If John can do it, why can't I?

Joseph

*23 October 1843*

Dear Gran,

The hound on the loose. Remember Mr. Blount, who whisper in Lulu's ear? Well, last week Lulu is sweeping the yard behind the house. Blount come out, rip up a sheet of paper, and scatter the pieces on the ground.

Lulu gather the scraps, give them to the cousin's children. They piece it together and read it, say it is a draft of a letter to Dr. Norcom.

Blount write that Mama be easy to catch, cause she come from Long Island every Sunday to see Lulu in Brooklyn. The letter even give Norcom the street address. They is only one other servant in the house. He colored too, so he help Lulu out. Tell her he seen the brother leave with an envelope in his hand, headed toward the post office.

Next day when Mama visit, Lulu tell her all about it. Mama then go back to Long Island. The white lady she work for want to help out. She go to an antislavery lawyer and a judge, ask them for advice.

They tell her about New York laws. Seems like police

in that state don't look for runaways as a rule. But if a slaveholder take his case to court and win, the police got to find the fugitive. Massachusetts is different. A few months back this state pass a new law. Can't no police here catch a slave. Can't no jail hold one.

So Mama is written to John. Want him to come get her and Lulu, if the Tredwells will let Sister go.

John throw a change of clothes in a satchel early this morning. "Uncle," I beg while he pack, "let me go along. The Tredwells don't have much money. They might want to sell Lulu, won't let her leave. I could grab her hand, snatch her away!"

"God forbid that Norcom tracks down your mother," John reply. "But if he does, he might kidnap Lulu, too, just for the pleasure of tormenting Harriet. For her sake, she must know that one of her children is safe."

"Uncle, don't it cost Norcom money to come up here after Mama? How come that old devil keep after her?"

John buckle the straps on his bag, shake his head. "When I was Norcom's office assistant, I saw many instances of his sick mind. The dark, restless moods he relieved with shots of painkiller. The mental confusion that followed. The rage he could ease only with another dose. Now his sickness is pointed at your mother like a pistol."

So here I sit in Boston, Gran. Nothing to do but knock the banjar and read Uncle John's geography book. And wish I could knock James Norcom ten miles to the other side of hell.

Your Joseph

---

*25 October 1843*

Dear Gran,

I got one big piece of news and one fat question. First, everybody in Boston now, safe and sound. Mama and Lulu seem wore out when they come in the door. Mama take off her hat, ease into a chair, and hold Lulu by her side. I bring her a cup of tea, but she don't let go of Sister long enough to drink it.

Lulu keep her head on Mama's shoulder, though I am glad to say she seem well. Her eyes is clear as May, and she is wearing a flannel skirt that Mama cut from her own skirt so Sister be warm while traveling.

John carry everybody's bags up the stairs. Then he and Mama collect they thoughts, tell me about the trip.

"When I arrived in Brooklyn," Uncle say, "the Tredwells insisted I bring Louisa back in ten days. I kept quiet and let them assume I would."

That make me laugh, Gran. The Tredwells got a long wait ahead of them.

"When John and your sister reached Long Island," Mama say, "we left immediately on the steamship."

Then Mama tell how the stewardess on the ship order them to sleep outside on the deck. She say that wealthy people below don't want to mix with coloreds.

"Outside in late October!" I cry. "That's worse than sleeping by the boiler room!"

"I spoke to the captain," Mama went on. "He must have guessed we were fugitives and took pity on us. Or maybe it was your sister's pleasing face that softened his heart."

I grin at Lulu, and she give me a weak smile back.

"Whatever the reason," Mama say, "he let us sleep in the berths below. When we arrived in Connecticut, I followed the judge's warning. We took a train route to Boston that few Southerners travel."

Lulu finally find her voice, say real proud, "The conductor let us ride in the very first train car!"

After that, I show Lulu my banjar, sing her a tune or two. She relax a bit, and we even dance a jig, show off for Mama and John. Then I take Lulu off to the corner. "Sister, I ain't said nothing about your secret to a living soul."

"I already tell Mama about the drinking," she reply, "but not the wicked words."

"Why not?"

Lulu sneak a quick look at Mama. "She don't need anything reminding her of the past."

I stare at Lulu, wonder what she mean.

"Don't you know?" she ask. "Norcom do the same to Mama when she living with his family. That's why she hide under Gran's roof all those years."

"Sister, how you learn such a thing?"

"One time I overhear Gran and Mark. They whispering about Norcom, and how he beat Mama when she would not kiss him."

So that is my question, Gran. How come you know all this and never tell me? You say, "Joseph, act like a man," but you don't treat me like one!

Well, I tell Lulu it don't seem possible the high-headed doctor would stoop so low. Why he wanting Mama's kisses when he got a wife of his own?

Before she can answer, Mama and John call for another jig. The thought of Norcom touching Mama make my face hot. But I hide it as best I can, shake a leg with Lulu. So they is dances and smiles tonight, as this is the first time we all been together since I can remember.

When slavery end, Gran, you better stuff two turkeys and set out your best plates. Cause we coming home, and I am bringing my question with me. Until then, you got time to think on the answer.

Your Joseph

# Great-Uncle Mark

*1 February 1844*

Dear Mark,

I am four feet, six inches tall, and almost fourteen. So I be writing you now, since you a man too. I hope you been taking care of your wife like you said you would, and looking in on Gran every day.

You won't believe how cold it is in Boston! The harbor is froze solid ten miles out. Thousands of people is on the ice this minute, skating along under the full moon.

But I am cooped up like a shoat in a pen. After Christmas, Uncle John decide I got too much time on my hands. He give me some of his books to study. I hate those arithmetic problems, but geography is all right, I guess.

John's geography book got a picture of a sea

monster. I am cutting it out and pasting it here, so you can see what whaling is all about.

The ship is in front of an iceberg. The spout of water, a course, is coming from the whale. The little boats is what sailors row out in when they ready to spear it. But this whale is rise right out of the water, flip one of the boats over. Hoo-ee! I wish I could get inside the picture, Mark. Do battle with a great monster of the sea!

I am fighting with these books instead. At least I got my own bed now. Last fall, Lulu and I move with Mama to the Widow Johnson's rooms. She live on Charter Street, near John's boardinghouse.

The widow need help with rent money. That's why Mama take in sewing to pay our part, make about $1.50 a week. She stay up late, strain her eyes with a needle and thread. Make me stay up too and read out loud to her.

Last week she decide I am going to the Smith School for colored children. Mama say she never had the chance for school learning, that her children must get all they can. She especially want me to work on my grammar. Stop saying "they" when I should say "there."

Mama will tutor Lulu at home every morning. Meantime, I walk twenty shivering blocks to the Smith School. I try to talk her out of it, but Mama, she got a powerful strong will.

Joseph

---

*12 March 1844*

Dear Mark,

I do not like the Smith School.

The place seem big enough at first. The building got three floors with a classroom on each one. But there is almost two hundred children in this place! The littlest sit in the basement. The older ones is crammed on the first and second floors. Got to perch on baby-size chairs, same as the basement children, 'cept our shanks hang off the sides.

Looking out the tall windows helps pass the time. So does looking at the girls. But none of us got a place to hang our coats, and the playground is only fifteen feet square. There's a high wall around it, like a jail yard. One of the older boys slip away while we outside today, didn't come back.

The teacher get mad, sure enough. He a white man name of Abner Forbes. He pinch the boys for punishment. Or he make them stand on one foot till their legs buckle. If Forbes get real mad at a boy, he whip the bottom of his feet. One time he even use a ruler on the back of a girl's hand. No telling what he might do to the poor fella who run out.

I tell Uncle John about Forbes. Uncle says it sickens him. That cruel white people who call themselves Christians should read their Bibles before mistreating coloreds.

A group of colored parents been having meetings about the school and how it is not as good as ones for white children. John been a time or two, but Mama keep to herself and never go.

Your great-nephew,
Joseph

*30 April 1844*

Dear Mark,

Snot running thick as buttermilk around here. Here's why.

Uncle John come over to see Mama this evening, and they sit outside on the stoop. Lulu and I upstairs, studying. When I hear talking, I step to the open window.

"Joseph!" whisper Lulu. "Private conversation should not interest you."

"Anything is more interesting than fractions," I whisper back.

John's voice is quiet at first. "Harriet, the parents are going to the school board about Forbes. If the group is large enough, their protest cannot be ignored. I urge you to come with me."

Mama sound weary. "Brother, the more the colored community sees of me, the more curious they will become about my past. Surely they already discuss the children's light skin."

When John's voice turn excitable, Lulu cannot help herself. She step to the window and listen too.

"So Samuel Sawyer still runs this family? Though I escaped from him four years ago? Though you are the mother of two children he won't claim in public as his own?"

My mouth drop open wide as a whale's. "Samuel Sawyer is our daddy!" I tell Lulu.

She nod, like she is known all along.

Mama start to weep. "Brother, I wouldn't change the past if I could. What I did was a great sin, but Samuel was nice to me. Being with him meant I could discourage Norcom's attentions. Besides, he gave me two loving children. I have been through too much to face the judgment of free coloreds in the North."

I guess John feel bad about upsetting Mama, cause he start blubbering with her.

That is when I grab Lulu by the arm. Shake her like she a rag rug. "Why is it," I ask, "everybody but me know about Sawyer?"

Lulu jerk away. "Remember when I go with Sawyer and his wife and baby to New York? The baby's nursemaid come too. She take me aside. Tells me that Sawyer is our daddy and make me promise never to repeat it. Anyway, Great-Uncle Mark been like a father to you, and Uncle John is like one now. Can't you forget about Sawyer?"

Then Sister turn weepy and run downstairs. My eyes water too, cause she is right about you helping raise me, Mark. But I wish Mama had think twice before picking a white man to be my daddy.

Joseph

---

*5 February 1845*

Dear Mark,

Snow everywhere, and more falling. I been under the covers in bed, reading over my letters to you. Only sad things happen since the last one. Seems like life is like the streets of this city—all slippery and uphill.

Last June the colored parents pass a resolution. It says children must stay away from the Smith School, cause of the teacher. Mama against pulling me out. But John insist, and he promise to help me with my studies.

He usually at the antislavery meetings, though. I'm mostly teaching my own self now. Trying to put an *s* on my words, and I ain't using "ain't" no more.

Joseph

---

*21 April 1845*

Dear Mark,

I'm fifteen years of age today. You wouldn't know it by Mama and John. Last night they put a leash on me.

"Son," Mama says, "saloons and dance halls are springing up throughout the North End. You mustn't roam so freely around this part of town. Especially at night."

I don't tell Mama and John that I been dreaming about a girl from Edenton. Maybe you know her, Mark. A right pretty gal name of Comfort, lives over at Hayes? She had the good sense to like me. Only trouble is, I didn't have the sense to like her back. Sometimes I go out hoping to meet up with a girl like her. I haven't found one yet, and I guess I never will.

John says, "It is time you earn some money. The words of Frederick Douglass are a warning to all of us. Learn a trade or starve!"

Then John tells me that he has meet a man who runs a printing business. And one of his employees, William Simmonds, plans to start his own newspaper at the end of the year.

"Simmonds will need an apprentice," Mama adds.

"Mama, I don't know nothing about printing!"

"But you will," she replies. "An apprentice works

for free until he is twenty-one. Then he hires himself out and earns money on his own."

"Work six years for free? I'm not doing it!"

"Oh, yes, you are," says John real quiet, his eyes stabbing mine.

Mama try to soothe me. She says John is joining lots of antislavery groups. Soon he be too busy to watch over me.

And her employer's wife is died. He's going to England in June, wants Mama to come along and mind his baby. When Mama gets home next spring, I will know a great deal about the printing trade, and that will make her proud.

"Well, Mama," I say, "after giving me a worthless white daddy, you disappear for years. Then you go north, run out on me again. So you got lots of practice leaving your children. Stay in England, see do I care!"

Mama catch her breath and bow her head, and John look like he might throttle me. I apologize right off for them harsh words, but I am still smoldering inside. A print shop is not one of Norcom's cornfields, but it seems like slavery all the same.

Joseph

*19 September 1845*

Dear Mark,

Mama gone to England, and I can't say I am sorry. We argue right up to the day she leave, mostly about the print shop, sometimes about the Irish. Thousands of them been pouring into the North End. They is begging for food on every corner. At night they shaking in cellars and sheds, sleeping on dirty straw. But Mama still think they better off than slaves.

So it's a good thing she gone, else we be picking each other to pieces. Cause now the papers is full of news about a plant blight in Ireland. It's turning the taters black. Since taters is mostly what the Irish eat, much of the country is starving to death. Those that can get away, do. Thousands more is pouring into Boston.

Tonight I visit Uncle John, talk to him about it. Ask him why Mama has always take such a hard stand on the Irish.

"After your mother escaped from Edenton by ship," he explain, "she went to New York by train. An Irish coachman at the station tried to cheat her. It left her with bad feelings."

"But John, that's just one man."

"It's a tangle, Joseph. A few years back, sixty

thousand Irish Americans signed a petition calling for the end of slavery. On the other hand, people in Boston are hiring Irish newcomers for low-paying jobs as servants and dock workers. Colored Americans can't find work."

John admit that he do not know what to think about the Irish. But he think the ones starving in Ireland is deserving of help, and so do I.

Joseph

---

*1 December 1845*

Dear Mark,

Today Uncle John tell me it's time to meet Mr. Simmonds, talk to him about my apprenticeship. I give John a black look, but it don't do any good.

Only one thing keeps me going. One time you say a man who don't keep his promise is no man at all. When I leave out of Edenton, I tell Gran we be together sometime. I mean to keep that promise.

After I earn a living as a printer, I'll offer Norcom so much money for Mama that he can't turn it down. Then I'll give Sawyer the five hundred dollars he pay for

Lulu and me, make him sign our free papers. Anything left over, I'll buy Gran a fine new shawl. On the day we meet again, I'll lay it round her shoulders myself.

Joseph

---

*2 December 1845*

Dear Mark,

You is live a lot longer than me and have meet lots of folks. But I bet you never meet a white man wearing a paper hat. Today I show up at the print shop where Mr. Simmonds still work. He come to the door with newspaper wrap around his head. Claims it keeps the ink from flying into his hair.

We stand outside the shop while he talks about his weekly newspaper. He's starting it at the end of the month.

"With the blessing of the Lord," says he, "I shall call it the *Saturday Rambler*. . . . Do you read Scripture, boy? Study it steadily, constantly, frequently! How do you spend your time? Never lose one moment, save to improve yourself!"

"I write letters," I reply, "and sometimes play the—"

"Letters! Splendid, splendid! I keep a daily journal

myself. Have done so for years. In this manner, I can track the time I've allotted to useful activities. In 1844, I attended one hundred thirty-eight religious meetings—in twenty-two months I never missed church, you know, except once when I lost my umbrella. I was present at Sabbath school fifteen times—never laugh or dance on the Lord's Day, young fellow—and I visited my mother on sixty-one occasions. I spent one hundred thirty-one evenings writing, fifty-four reading books, thirteen practicing music, and a total of six hours in amusements!"

Mark, I want to ask just what them amusements were. But Mr. William Simmonds never let me finish a sentence. Anyway, he's a preacher sort of man. He and I might not see eye-to-eye about amusements.

Joseph

---

*15 December 1845*

Dear Mark,

After all my fretting, the newspaper shop isn't so bad. One apprentice is about my age, a white boy name of Thomas. The other is an Irish American, name of Eugene. He's about thirteen, I think. Both is lively, and we get along fine.

Simmonds praises me, says I'm a quick learner. He's too high-talking, Mark, and an addle-brain sometimes. But he's all right, I guess. To thank me for working so hard, he give me a Bible. I have not got around to reading it.

So far, my job is mostly drop and stoop. Simmonds picks metal letters out of a case and puts them in a stick. When he drops a letter, I pick it up quicker than you can tap a toe. If I put them back in the right order, he can pluck the exact one he needs. Don't even have to look at the case.

After Simmonds fills the stick with words, he slides them into a heavy metal plate. The plate goes on the bottom of the press, which looks like a giant waffle iron.

Next Simmonds inks the plate. That's where Eugene comes in. Eugene cards dirty wool. When he gets a clean clump, he balls it up, wraps it in leather, and ties it to a stick.

Simmonds puts newspaper around his head, dips the ball in ink, and rolls it across the plate of type. I stand back then, cause ink flies everywhere, and I cannot feature myself wearing a paper hat.

Then Simmonds slips a piece of blank paper inside the lid of the waffle iron. He pulls a lever, squashes the paper down on the inked letters. And this is how he makes a printed page.

A printing press is something to see, Mark. It's a long way from tracing words in the mud back in Edenton, and lots faster.

Thomas's job is cleaning the floor. When Simmonds isn't looking, he waltzes with the brush mop. Today Eugene waits till Simmonds takes a tea break. He mats some scrap wool and makes a bonnet with it. Puts it on the brush head and ties his scarf underneath.

"She's a beaut, ain't she?" Eugene brags. "Prettier than any girl you'll ever get, Thomas, cause you're an ugly so-and-so."

Thomas grabs the mop and spins it round. "Give us a kiss, darlin'!" he croons, and lays a smooch on it.

These boys make me laugh, Mark. Too bad Mama is in England, or I would set her straight about the Irish.

Joseph

---

*9 March 1846*

Dear Mark,

A worse day I never knew in my life. It being the tail end of winter, with snow still on the ground, I bring my banjar to the shop. Think I'll play a little tune for the boys, lighten things up.

Simmonds steps out for dinner around noon. Soon as the door slams, Thomas commences to dance with his wooden girlfriend. I pull my banjar from the bag. Sing a verse of "Roustabout," but change the words a bit.

*Where did you get that pretty little scarf?*
*That hat you wear so fine?*
*I get the scarf from a print shop man . . .*

Thomas laughs, strokes the brush like it's hair. Eugene hollers, "Joseph, you ought to put on blackface!"

"That's right," says Thomas. "You could play in one of them minstrel bands. Do you know 'Fine Old Colored Gentleman'? I heard it just last week at a dance hall."

Thomas shuffles his feet and sings,

*His temper was very mild*
*When he was let alone,*
*But when you get him dander up*
*He spunk to de backbone*

Mark, I haven't seen a minstrel show. Mama won't let me go. But Uncle John went to one last year. He come home saying it's a disgrace.

White men and coloreds, too, smear their faces with burnt cork. Get up on stage, pretend to be slaves. They crack jokes that make colored people seem stupid. Singers usually on the stage too, along with musicians. Sometimes they play bones or tambourine, but always a banjar.

So when I hear the word minstrel, I glare at the boys, slip the banjar in its bag. About then, Simmonds comes back. Eugene and Thomas act all innocent, like they don't know they have insult my race. But Simmonds must have feel the heat in the air. He tells us to get back to work, stays close by us the rest of the day.

Maybe Mama right about the Irish, after all.

Joseph

---

*10 March 1846*

Dear Mark,

*Today* been the worst day of my life. This morning Simmonds pulls a piece of smelly goatskin from a box.

"Boys," he says, "it is time you learn to soften the skin for the ink ball. We call it treading the pelt."

He shows us how to scrape hair off the skin. "Next, relieve yourself in a jar," he explains with a broad smile, "and place the skin in it. Once a day, remove the skin. Knead it with your bare feet and place it back in the jar. Repeat until the skin is soft as a glove."

Simmonds tells us to choose who tries it first, then leaves the shop. I decide he's testing us, see can we get along after yesterday.

"Mother of God," Eugene cries. "Peeing in a jar!"

"Sweet Jaysus!" says Thomas.

I figure I will show them boys up.

"Oh, I'll do it," I say real easy. I hunt for a jar—a tall one, cause I don't want nothing splashing back on me.

"You boys is yellow as new chicks. Why, this is nothing compared to the teacher I had at the Smith School. He used to beat—"

Eugene gives a long, high whistle.

"The Smith School?" Thomas asks. "Ain't that for coloreds?"

"You sure fooled us," says Eugene. "No wonder you're so handy with the banjar!"

"I guess you know all about yellow," Thomas says. "High yellow. What kind of woolly hair you hiding under there?"

He snatches the cap from my head and stuffs it in his pocket. Then he starts sweeping wide loops around me. Eugene goes to his work table, sits with his back turned.

I go out the back door, do my business in the jar. Drop in the goatskin, come inside, and place it careful on the shelf. By the time Simmonds returns, I'm straightening letters in the case, sweet as you please.

Somebody's hand will dip in my pee tomorrow, but it won't be mine.

Joseph

---

*11 March 1846*

Dear Mark,

I wander in circles around the North End today. Listen to the gulls cry, "Uh oh, uh oh," and try to understand this thing. Does Mister Simmonds know or care that them white boys abuse me so bad? Or maybe he thinks I'm white, and that's why he been nice to me.

Well, it don't matter now. I never meet my great-uncle Joseph, but I know this. We got more in common than our names. Gran tell me one time he would not be treated like a dog. Me neither.

Last week I help Simmonds set type for an advertisement. It say thousands of men is needed in New Bedford for whaling crews, that ships sail out of there every day.

The cars for New Bedford leave at seven thirty a.m. Come morning, I'll be on that train. And I'm leaving my banjar behind.

Joseph

# *Part* III

## The Sea

1846–1849

# Uncle John

NEW BEDFORD, MASSACHUSETTS
*18 March 1846*

Dear Uncle John,

Don't I wish I could mail this letter! But you might come down here to drag me back, and I cannot stomach Boston again.

I guess by now you seen the note I left Lulu about the print shop. Maybe I been mean, sneaking off without saying where I'm headed. But I figure Widow Johnson can take care of Sister till Mama gets back from England. Besides, it's best this way. If Simmonds comes looking for me, you can say for true you don't know where I am.

New Bedford is a hurry-scurry town, Uncle. Lots more colored people than Boston. I find a boardinghouse right off. It's six blocks up the hill from the water. Own by a colored man name of Moses Shepherd. He takes me upstairs, shows me a room the size of a pantry. Got only a bed, a dresser, and a cracked looking glass on the wall.

"What you running from, boy?" he asks.

"Lots of things," I answer. "White boys in Boston wanting my pride. White man in North Carolina wanting my flesh."

"Well, you come to the right place. Most whites in this city would shelter a runaway. You got rent money?"

"I spend my last shilling on the train ticket."

"Then go to the docks," Shepherd orders, "and get a job."

All week I been hauling barrels of whale oil off ships. The first night my muscles scream like they been hammered. Unloading them barrels is the hardest work I ever done. Stinky, too. Whale oil got the smell of ripe fruit been sitting too long.

Tonight I take a bath, try to get rid of the stench. Don't do much good. The water is gray from five boarders who use it before me . But while I scrub, I think about my plan. I come here to be a sailor, make freedom money. Now I believe I can earn enough on the docks without stepping foot on a ship.

Think of it, Uncle! No more Norcom or Sawyer for

our family to worry about. Maybe that will make up for taking your books without asking.

Your nephew,
Joseph

---

*30 June 1846*

Dear Uncle John,

No time lately for reading or writing. I been staying up till midnight, playing cards. Men here at the boardinghouse is teaching me. Them sailors hail from all over the world. So many strange places, I had to look them up in your geography book: the Azore Islands, Cape Verde Islands, Australia, Sandwich Islands. Seems like these fellas know every card game there is. Whist is their favorite, though, and they play for money.

Uncle, if I can just win a time or two, I can add to my earnings, be that much closer to paying Norcom and Sawyer. Only thing is, I lose more than I win. That is call being in the hole. But don't you worry. I be getting out soon enough. I just need more practice.

Joseph

*27 July 1846*

Dear Uncle John,

I'm so deep in the hole, can't see the top. It's bad enough losing my own freedom money. The shame is losing Mama's and Lulu's, too.

This morning I overhear Mr. Shepherd fussing at the other boarders. "The boy is too young for gambling. You let him play again, I'll call off all the games."

I decide I'll wait till tonight when Shepherd is asleep, try and win my losings back. But after supper, a Mr. Chase strolls into the dining room. He's wearing the tallest black hat and finest black suit I ever seen.

"Good evening, sailors!" Chase says. He lays his hat real careful on the table, unbuttons his jacket, and sits down. "I'm the agent for a small whaling bark called the *Ivy Ann*. Every sailor who signs up receives protection papers and seventy-five dollars in clothes."

Chase pulls out a stack of printed slips, slaps them on the table. "Line up, if you please!"

I figure it's time I earn some real money, and free

clothes sound fine too. After a few men get in line, I join them. When my turn come, I ask, "What exactly is a protection paper, Mr. Chase?"

"Every colored sailor in America has to have one," he replies. "Even a free man. It protects him from slave hunters if he goes ashore at a Southern port. Otherwise, he could be locked up and sold."

Then Chase asks, "What's your name, boy? Where were you born?"

"Joseph Jacobs. Edenton, North Carolina."

"Age?"

Figure I best make that number higher, Uncle. Otherwise, the captain might pick me to be his cabin boy, and I want to be a real sailor.

"Seventeen," I reply.

"Height?"

"Five feet."

Chase fills in my answers. When he gets to the one that says color, he writes in "light."

Then he stops, looks up. Frowns while he crosses out "light" and writes in "dark." He hands me the paper, and I fold it, go straight to my room. Stare at the looking glass to see what's in there.

I can't tell if the person staring back is brown, white, yellow, light, or dark. Truth is, I don't hardly know who Joseph Jacobs is anymore.

Joseph

*12 August 1846*

Dear Uncle John,

First of the month, Mr. Chase give me the new clothes. Checked shirt, loose trowsers, canvas hat, oilcloth suit, and a short jacket that makes me look like a trained monkey. Chase is right generous, cause he give me a knife, spoon, and tin cup, too. Plus a sea chest to store everything.

Next day I show up at the dock, sign a paper. It says I get 1/188 of all profit from the trip. One hundred eighty-eight times all the profit—that's a lot, Uncle!

I wish I had ask you more about whaling when I had the chance. I never knew that sailors got to sleep stacked in wooden berths in the forecastle. Cap'n Jordan and his officers all cozy in their cabins mid-deck. The cooper and carpenter and cabin boy sleep in smaller rooms in the belly of the ship.

But we sailors is tight as minnows in a space about twelve by twelve. We got only one little hatch for light and fresh air. The butt of the mast pole takes up what floor room there is.

And how come nothing goes by its real name on a whaler? Starboard is right, larboard is left. A sailor's pay is his lay. His sea chest a donkey. The forecastle is the fo'c'sle. And old hands who already been to sea call themselves fishy men. They call new fellas like me greenies.

These past ten days, the greenies been packing every cranny of this ship with food, water casks, harpoons, wood staves for fifteen hundred barrels—everything we might need for three years. I don't got much to call my own. My books, the new clothes, and this ledger is all. They fit in the donkey with room to spare.

It's a good thing we sailors got donkeys, cause there's no room for chairs in the fo'c'sle. First night on ship, the sailors perch on their chests and introduce themselves.

Five of the six fishy men—four coloreds, two whites—is from the Northern states. But one colored, name of Isaac, says he's from Virginia. He got a rake of thick white scars on the left side of his head. The lines is so deep, looks like a hag been scratching him. Make me wonder what his story is, but I decide it's none of my business.

The other greenies is all white boys from Nantucket or New Bedford. Some friendly, some not so. When everybody done with introductions, only one fella is left. His skin mahogany brown, and he got a voice coarse as pepper.

"Luis, from Cabo Verde," says he.

"An Afrikey man!" says as Irish greenie, name of Owen.

Luis mutters, "Never stepped foot in Africkey. Cabo Verde three hundred miles off the coast. My mother African. She slave on one of the islands. My father, he Portuguese slave trader. He buy her, marry her."

Owen blurts, "Sure, and it's African you're looking to me!" His words come out funny, like he's wrapping his tongue three times around each one.

"And you talk like a mick," Luis replies. "A dirty potato digger . . ." He curses and spits a line of tobaccy juice straight in Owen's eye. The fishy men roar, slap their knees laughing.

Owen tries to lunge at Luis, but he gets to coughing. It's a hacking sound, like his lungs is chewed up. I feel right sorry for him at first. Then I figure an Irish boy is of no interest to me anyway.

Joseph

---

*1 October 1846*

Dear Uncle John,

You never tell me how the ship lurches up and down when it moves through rough seas. Or that sailors' stomachs lurch too. Now I know why they call us greenies. All us new boys been the color of creek slime these past weeks. Got nothing left to throw up.

I'm not long for this world. If ever you see this letter, tell Mama I passed over near the Azores. Tell her I said good-bye.

Joseph

---

*15 October 1846*

Dear Uncle John,

The seasickness is eased some, but I'm terrible sorry I come on this trip.

Cap'n surprises us most every week. Calls, "Man the boats!" Then we greenies run to a whaler, lower it in the water, and row after a pretend whale. Between drills, sailors scrub the decks or scrape the decks or paint the decks. When we not on our hands and knees, we doing something or other to the sails. Climbing mast poles to tie the sails down. Climbing up to unfurl them. So many sails, ropes, knots, all with different names.

At night Cook brings us food in a wooden tub he calls a kid. Sailors get nothing but salt pork, salt pork, salt pork. Sometimes Cook livens things up, brings more salt pork.

Tomorrow I stand my first watch in the crow's nest. When I look up at that platform, I near about cry. Sharks usually follow the *Ivy Ann*. One big roll of the ship, I might fall a hundred feet into the water. Them sharp teeth could chop me into slaw!

Joseph

---

*16 October 1846*

Dear Uncle John,

I'm still in one piece—for now, anyway. Captain's third mate is a fella name of Tom Morgan. He sends Owen up to the crow's nest first. Tells me to watch how the mick climbs the rope ladders.

Morgan got pocky skin and greasy hair long as a cow switch. He don't look like somebody to argue with, so I watch real careful when Owen scuttles up the rigging. His long, bony arms stretch up from line to line, and his feet hug the cross ropes like he a lizard. Ten seconds later he's waving from the crow's nest.

Morgan gives me a shove, and I start up. "Don't look down, and don't stop!" he calls. "Keep your eyes on your hands!"

Twenty feet up, the rope is burning my palms. Forty feet, my arm muscles is shaking with the strain. Eighty feet, my breath is near gone.

Two minutes later I wiggle through a little hatch on the platform and am standing up straight. Feeling right proud of myself too.

I hold tight to the iron bar circling the mast pole, squint down at the deck. Morgan looks no bigger to my eye than a rat. The sight makes me dizzy, brings me down on my knees. I hunch over, whisper, "Mama, Mama."

Owen is next to me inside his own iron circle. "Think about beans!" he screams over the wind. "Baked beans are my favorite! But any sort will do!"

This Irish boy is crazy, I think, but next thing I know, I'm remembering Gran's snap beans. How she used to boil a mess of them with a hunk of fatback, salt them up good. That takes my mind off where I am. Before long, I'm on my feet again, gawping at the blanket of deep green sea.

"How come you love beans so much?" I shout.

"First meal I had in Amerikay was a bowl of steaming baked beans. I'll never forget it!"

"And how come you end up on a whaler?"

"I found a job sweeping floors in a mill near Boston. Hated being cooped up. Whaling was a chance to get free of the place!"

"You got any family?"

Owen turn his freckly face toward the sea, and the wind swoop his words away. He don't say nothing else while we search the waves.

We spy an albatross bird flying like a goose. Flying fish that soar like birds. Dolphins that look to be smiling. But no sign of a whale spouting its spray high in the air.

Joseph

---

*20 October 1846*

Dear Uncle John,

Cap'n Jordan is worried. Says if we don't spot a whale soon, the hair will fall from his head. That's something I'd like to see. Cap'n is six feet tall, with a scowly face. He got enough black hair for two men, and a scratchy beard to boot.

After supper, I go down to the fo'c'sle, but the stink of old vomit turns my stomach. I join Isaac on deck while he mans the wheel. Morgan is the officer on watch. He strolls the foredeck, comes back now and again to check the compass.

I stare at the stars, glinty as new coins. Wonder how many miles is between me and Norcom.

When Morgan walks off a ways, I ask real low, "Isaac, is you a free man or slave?"

"Trying to be free," he answers. "Seven years ago, massa slap me up side the head with a pitchfork. Don't nobody hit Isaac more than once. I beat him good. Stole a knife off him, greased my feet with soap, and started running."

"He come after you?"

"I heard his hound dogs, but the soap hid the scent. Took me four months to get from Virginia to Boston. This is my third whaling trip. When it's over, I'll have enough to buy a little three-acre farm in Maine. I hear they let coloreds live in peace up there. Being massa of my own land—that's being free."

"What if Cap'n finds out you on the run?" I ask.

"That's why I picked the *Ivy Ann*," Isaac explains. "Captains usually make a list of their sailors. But Jordan's a Quaker, and most don't hold with slavery. Cap'n don't make a list. That way, if he's carrying fugitive sailors, nobody can trace them."

We stare out over the inky water for a while, listen to the sails *whoomp* in the night breeze. Morgan comes back, checks the compass. Calls, "Left to larboard! Steer a course south by southeast!"

Isaac grips the knobs on the wheel tighter, pushes to the left.

"Color don't matter so much out here on the sea, does it?" I ask when Morgan wanders off.

"Matters more at home, that's true. Lots more. But listen, boy, you light enough to pass for white when you get back on land. Cover that wavy hair with a cap, you could fool most folks."

"Already fooled them twice," I say, "without even trying."

"Well, that's a sign, then. Just remember," Isaac warns, "if you pass all the time, you be living a lie every hour of your life. Can you give up your family, or see them only in secret? It's something to think about."

About then, I notice a blank spot in the sky. "Isaac, some of the Big Dipper handle is gone!"

"We three thousand miles south of home. You won't see all the northern stars down here."

Uncle, the Dipper handle always been the road to Mama in my mind. Now that it's disappearing, feels like I might never see her again. But if ever I do, I won't ever give her up, or you or Lulu, either. Not for anything.

Joseph

*21 October 1846*

Dear Uncle John,

Today Morgan pairs me up with Owen. Tells us to coat the water casks with tar, keep the wood from rotting. It's tedious work. I figure I best talk to him, Irish or not, else die of boredom. I ask him, "Is there ghosts in Ireland?"

Owen dips his brush in a pot of black goo. Squats down to reach the bottom stave. "Oh, indeed. Frightful spirits live all about in trees and caves."

"Huh," I brag. "That's not near so bad as a plat eye."

We give the barrel a turn, and I tell Owen about shape changers. How they got ugly eyes and chase people through the night.

"Truly, were ye ever seeing a plat eye?" Owen asks. He stands for a stretch.

"Naw," I admit. "My granny tell them stories to make me behave."

"Your granny . . . what about your ma?"

Before I know it, I have tell Owen about Gran, Lulu, and Mark. How you been whaling before, Uncle, and is now an abolitionist. That I aim to buy my family's freedom. It feel good to talk about the plans. Owen seem to understand the hardness of it all.

When I tell how Norcom come after Mama, Owen nod.

"Your doctor," says he, "and my English landlord are one of a kind. When the potatoes went black, we couldn't pay rent on the cottage. One day, redcoat English soldiers showed up. Violent fellows, they were. They smashed the door and flung everything out. Then they set fire to the roof."

"With all y'all still in there?" I cry.

"Aye. They smoked us out. Me little brother and sister were already in the ground from the hunger. Ma and Da saw no reason to stay. That morning they were off to Dublin, hoping to beg scraps of food along the road. Begging was not for me. I never saw them again."

Then Owen tells how he poach deer from the landlord's estate and sell the meat to buy his ship ticket. He bring a sack of oaten cakes with him on the journey. But he near dead by the time he eat that first bowl of baked beans in Boston.

"I miss me family, especially the wee ones," Owen says. "What about your da? You haven't mentioned him."

"He a white man name of Sawyer. Never been a real daddy to me."

"Ah, that's where your white blood comes from," says Owen.

Uncle, something about them words set a fire in my head. I hear Josiah saying, "Joseph, you're as white as I am." And Eugene saying, "I guess you know all about yellow."

"I'm not white, you scrawny mick!" I shout. "Or yellow, or light, or dark. I'm nothing but my own self!"

I take a swing at Owen, smash my fist in his nose. He falls to the deck, blood sliding to his mouth. "Jaysus," says he, "I didn't mean anything by it! But if it's a fight you're wanting, I'll not deny ye!"

He bounds up, slices into my lower lip. Before I can swing again, Morgan comes along.

"Fifteen barrels left," he says. "Finish by sunset, or I'll bring out the whip. Then you'll see real blood."

Owen and I work on through the afternoon, silent as snakes. When quitting time come, we stop to clean the brushes in spirits. I sneak a glance at him.

"Your nose still bleeding some," I say.

"So's your lip," he answers. "I'm not Norcom, Joseph. Or Sawyer, either. I'm my own self too."

Owen offers his hand. "Friends?"

"White boys can't be friends to coloreds. Friendly, maybe, never friends."

"This one can. You'll see."

I shake his hand. *Yes,* I'm thinking, *I always do see.*

Joseph

*25 October 1846*

Dear Uncle John,

I believe a piece of Luis's mind is split off. Tonight in the fo'c'sle he sips rum from a bottle he been hiding in his donkey. Gets a loose tongue, commences to tell the story of a whaling ship called the *Essex*.

"Thirty year ago," says Luis, "great white whale stove it in, broke it up. Crew go off in five boats. Soon they starving."

Luis howls with laughter, takes a swig. "When one man die, the rest eat him. Second man die, eat him, too!"

"Starving is no way to die," Owen says between coughs. He leans over, puts his hands on his knees to steady himself. "And 'tis indecent to devour the flesh of the dead."

"What you worry about?" says Luis, wiping a dribble from his mouth. "Nobody here would eat stringy Irish mick."

By now, Owen's pale face is splotchy red. "Or greasy Portugee," says he.

Luis stands, rolls his wad around, and loads up his mouth with brown juice. I step between him and Owen.

"Don't try it," I warn Luis. "I won't spend three years with a spitting fool."

When the ship rolls, the oil lantern over Luis's head swings from its chain. His eyeballs turn yellow, black, yellow in the flickering light.

"Beware, little milk-and-molasses man," he says to me, low and mean. "At least one sailor die on every whaling trip."

He moves his fingers to his belt, strokes the handle of a knife hanging in its sheath. I stare at the knife, wish I was anywhere but trapped on a ship with a cuckoo bird.

For one second nobody stirs, cause these is small quarters for such a big threat. Owen jumps up, takes hold of the sheath with one hand. With the other, he twists the neck of Luis's shirt.

"One sailor dies?" Owen asks. "We could make that two."

He pushes his thumb into Luis's gullet and lets go. Stands back, fists raised and breathing hard.

Luis is stuck, cause he got to fight or give in.

"Oh, sit down, Luis," says Isaac. "You don't got the sense of a turnip."

Everybody laughs, and that eases the strain. To save face, Luis spits at Owen's feet. Then he climbs in his berth. Half a minute later, the bully is asleep.

In a few days we landing off Brava, one of the Cape Verde Islands. Cap'n and Morgan is going ashore to buy fruit and casks of fresh water. Thinking about oranges makes my mouth juices run, and Cook says they'll keep our gums from bleeding. But if everybody on them islands is like Luis, I'd as soon sail on by.

Joseph

---

*28 October 1846*

Dear Uncle John,

When the sun come up at four this morning, it's already eighty degrees. As I'm stripping off the monkey jacket, Isaac calls, "Look smart, Joseph! We cross the equator today."

"The what?"

"The line going around the middle of the earth. It's like a belt. You can't miss it." Isaac chuckles like he's telling the best joke in the world.

Well, I'm staring through the hazy air, but I don't see no belt in the water.

Then the first mate yells, "We've crossed the line!"

That's when Luis comes up behind Owen. Blindfolds him with a neck scarf, forces a cup of saltwater down him.

"Celebration time!" Luis screams. "You push finger in my throat, I push this down yours!"

Owen gags, and Cap'n roars out of his cabin. "Halt!" he orders. "I'll have no more of that foolery on my vessel, else you'll feel the bite of Morgan's whip."

Luis unties the blindfold, but Owen is choking so bad, he got to go below, lay in his berth.

Tonight, Cap'n sends a round of rum down to the fo'c'sle, lets us party cause we cross the line. The sailors get right giddy, clear a spot around the mast pole. One of them saws on his fiddle while the others dance jigs. I kick a leg, till I see how Luis is watching Owen. Giving him the crazy eye like he got another trick in mind.

I move over, sit on Owen's donkey. Hand him water when the coughing grabs him. Tomorrow I'm telling the Cap'n he don't look so good. That lately a few drops of blood been flying from his mouth.

Joseph

---

*1 November 1846*
*Eight p.m.*

Dear Uncle John,

A long day, and not over yet. It start at dawn, when I tap on the door of Jordan's cabin. "Begging your pardon, sir. Owen feeling poorly. Got a hard cough, don't breathe easy."

Cap'n frowns. "I can't spare a man to illness. Does the cough produce blood?"

"A little, sir. And he awful pale under them freckles."

Cap'n steps inside, comes out with an eyedropper of laudanum. "Mix one drop with a cup of water. Give him a little at a time."

I go below, do like Cap'n says. "Drink it slow," I tell Owen.

Just then we hear the call everybody been waiting for. "Thar she blows! Right whale, Cap'n!"

"Where now?" Cap'n calls.

"Three points to the starboard bow! Two miles away, headed windward!"

Owen hears the stampede of feet above and tries to climb over the wooden guard of his berth. "Aye, Joseph! A-whaling we'll go at last!"

I shove him back in. "You too sick to lift a spoon," I say, "much less an oar."

I climb the hatch ladder and race to boat number one. All four boats row for two hours, but we don't see nothing. Then, with a great swooshing sound, the beast splits the surface twenty feet from my side, and a powerful splash soaks us clear through. I don't have to tell you, Uncle, I'm thinking my end is near.

"Quiet, now," Morgan whispers from the stern.

We slip our oars in the water, soft as cutting warm butter. Soon we is next to the whale. Luis is standing at the bow with his harpoon, and it's tied to a long rope wound inside a tub. He draws himself up, darts the thing in the whale's fleshy side.

"Fasto!" Luis cries.

Well, that whale is mad, and rightly so. He kicks and rolls, sets off through the water fast as a ship at full sail. All the while, the rope unwinds and holds us to him. We fly along behind till the monster tires out.

As you know, Uncle, it's the custom for the officer to kill the whale. Morgan and Luis grab our heads for balance while they change places. Then I pitch Morgan a lance. We row nigh to the whale's giant head, and Morgan buries it deep inside. More blood than ever I see in my life floods from that poor whale's snout.

When his huge tail slams the water, Morgan screams, "Back, back!"

We back-paddle till we safe from the flip. For an hour the creature makes death spirals in the red water. Up we row to it again. Morgan aims another lance straight into one of his staring eyes. When the carcass lays still, the deed is done.

We drag the giant dead thing five miles to the *Ivy Ann*, find the other boats waiting for us. Them sailors take over. Put a chain around the whale's tail, haul it up to a stage rigged on the side of the ship.

Cap'n orders the sailors in my boat to go below, rest a while. We too tired for sleep. Owen been pestering us with questions, but nobody answer. Some of us is writing in journals. Isaac is carving a picture of the *Ivy Ann* on a whale tooth.

And I'm thinking hard about what you say back in Boston, Uncle. That I should leave whaling alone. I wish I had listen. Chasing flesh for money is evil work. Makes me feel like I have turn into Norcom.

Joseph

---

*2 November 1846*
*Ten a.m.*

Dear Uncle John,

The other sailors work all night. Cut blubber into strips five feet wide, twenty feet long. Slice them thick as steaks, then thin as paper. The pieces is boiled in big brick ovens to separate the oil from the flesh. Uncle, you right about the stench of blubber and blood. It's soaked into everything and everywhere on board.

At dawn Morgan calls down the hatch, "Rouse yourself, boys! That greasy oil is cooling, and I need all yer sweet little hands. Some to ladle it in barrels, some to haul barrels to the hold."

Amidst a grumble of curses, we turn out of our berths. I take a quick look at Owen. He can't even sit up, got spots red as rouge on his cheeks.

"You lazy hog," I joke.

He looks at me with eyes too bright by far.

"What some people won't do to skip work. Hold on. I'll get more of Jordan's fancy water."

This time Cap'n brings the laudanum himself. "His fever is dangerously high," says Jordan. "Stay with him until he falls asleep."

Owen tosses a while, mumbles fever curses at some English soldier. After a time, he sits himself up. Digs his fingers in my arm like he's in a hurry.

"Joseph," he asks, "would you be telling me one thing? What's it like to be colored? The everydayness of it, not just the slavery part."

I shake off his hand. "You trying to pick another fight? What's it like to be white?"

"I never thought about it. I only kept out of the Englishman's way."

"Being white means never being on the run," I say.

Owen falls back with a rattling sigh. "Everybody's on the run from something."

"Not as fast as colored folks," I cry. "And not forever!"

"Aye," Owen answers, "but me parents are likely

dead in a ditch by now. Even on the run, you've got a family. If I could be you, I would."

A white boy wanting to be me! The thought make me laugh. "You don't know what you're saying, Owen! Slavery is scattered my family like catkins. None of us got a real home except Gran, and she's in a slave state we can't go back to."

"Two of you in one place, wherever it is. That's home."

He tries to say more, but blood sprays out.

Uncle, the ship is pitching hard now. The timbers is creaking bad, like God snapping twigs. We in such a heavy swell, I can't hold this pencil straight. . . .

*Ten p.m.*

A lifetime gone by since the storm start. When the ship roll heavy to one side, Owen almost falls from his berth. I roll him back in.

"Remember what Luis said?" he asks.

"I never pay no mind to Luis. Listen, can you hear Cap'n? He's calling the men to furl all sails. We must be in for it!"

The ship heaves up forty degrees. All the donkeys slide to one end of the fo'c'sle with a crash. I grab a rope from a peg, lift Owen's skinny bones. Loop it around his chest and hips. Tie one end to the mast pole, the other to the peg.

I see Owen's lips moving and lean over. "Luis said . . . Luis said . . . one man dies on every whaling trip. Ye might be looking at him."

"Aw, don't think about that now," I say. "Think about beans!"

Owen says something else, but I can't make it out. I'd like to think it was laughing I hear.

"I'm going above!" I yell. "See can I help!"

When I get on deck, pewter-colored clouds is rushing straight at us. In less than a minute, we is in the black mouth of the storm, and it's tossing the *Ivy Ann* like a toy. Waves big as houses rise up, disappear, and rise again.

"Lash the topgallant sails!" Cap'n calls. I look up through the stinging rain, see Isaac creep along the ropes. He can't do it alone, I think.

I swallow my bile, scramble up them ropes. Isaac and I hang over the mast pole, flapping like towels on a line. When a strong gust about blows me off, he grabs me by the collar, catches me before I fall. Somehow we lash the canvas, then shimmy down. Try to help the others save what's left of the whale flesh, but it all wash overboard.

The gale rages another four hours, and quick as it come, it blow on by. Though we still trapped in fog, the water is glassy smooth. Every last man of us is bushed, out of breath. Even Jordan's face is showing pale under his beard. He finds me resting by the ovens, asks how Owen is.

"Sleeping, most likely," I pant. "I give him a stiff dose, then tie him in."

"Check on him."

I go below, see that Owen is still fast asleep. I stumble into my berth, too tired to untie him. A few minutes ago, Luis wake me. "The mick is sleeping, all right," he crow. "But he ain't never waking up!"

Joseph

# Owen

*28 February 1847*

Dear Owen,

For three months I have pick up this pencil. Then I throw it down. Study my Uncle John's books instead. Learn more grammar and geography, and arithmetic, too, when I can stand it. Anything to keep from thinking how you die alone. Tonight I'm ready to recollect it all.

Luis surprise me the day we bury you. When he slip off your clothes, I holler, "Don't touch him! You the one make him sick!"

"Boy already had consumption," Luis reply. "Now clear off. Got to lay dead to rest, even white one. Don't, it bad luck."

"Where I come from, folks plant a tree on the grave."

"Tree." Luis snorts. "You no help, boy."

He takes a shirt from his donkey, says, "This what we do on Brava."

He rips it in four strips, ties your limp limbs together, Owen. I help him re-dress you, and we carry you to the deck.

Isaac and Morgan sew you inside a sail, then Cap'n says a few prayers. Meantime, Luis turns over the wooden kid, makes it into a drum. While Cap'n and Isaac slide you over the bulwarks, Luis beats that kid.

"Torna!" he wails. "Torna!"

I head up to the bow. Stare into the briny water and picture you down there with the sharks. Isaac soon joins me. "What's Luis wailing back there?" I ask.

"Some kind of funny mix of Portuguee and African. It means return to dust."

"Dust. You mean fishbait."

"I know he been your friend," Isaac says.

"He's no friend. He died on me. Betrayed me, just like every other white boy I know."

"White boys same as colored, Joseph—all dead in the end. It's what we do when we here that matters."

Well, Owen, you stood up to Luis for me, I'll give you that. And you did wonder what it's like to be me. Even wanted to be me. That's something no other white boy ever done. So I want you to know I'm forgiving you for dying. And I forgive you for leaving me to climb the masthead alone.

Since you pass over, every sailor got to stand

double watch, eight hours at a stretch. Sometimes the fear comes back on me bad, like today. I squinch down, think I might as well jump and get the falling over with. Then I spy shark fins slicing the water below. That clear my head real quick.

Cap'n swears the double watches won't last forever. Says he'll add more crew when we reach Sydney, Australia. The ship is making two hundred miles a day—the fastest since we left New Bedford. We slow down when we round the Cape of Good Hope. Soon as we hit the Indian Ocean, we pick up swift winds.

Every week or so, we spear a whale. The other sailors keep track by drawing pictures in their journals. I'm doing the same, so you can know what's going on. A few of the monsters get away from us. Most is not so lucky. I can't get used to killing them or standing ankle-deep in blood while we cook out the blubber. But it's got to be done.

We already fill five hundred barrels with oil. The sooner we fill the other thousand, the sooner we head home. Captain says maybe we'll have a short, greasy journey, after all, and that's the finest whaling trip there is. With one sailor on the *Ivy Ann* gone, I figure it's too late for a fine trip. All I want is the pay waiting at the end.

Joseph

---

*12 March 1847*

Dear Owen,

We pick up two new sailors in Sydney this week. English fellas. Isaac says they're ex-convicts, sent to Australia to serve their term. After what you tell me about the English, I stay clear of them.

This morning Morgan put Luis and me to scraping varnish on the bulwarks. We get to talking, if you can call it that. You might remember that Luis is like a door. Sometimes his hinges get terrible loose.

"Luis," I say, "I got to ask you something. You hate Owen from the start. How come?"

Luis dips his cup in a bucket of stale water. "Got no use for greenies. Specially white ones can't tell difference between African and Portuguese."

"That's not enough to hate somebody."

"And what he know about starvation?" ask Luis.

"He did," I argue, "he did!"

Luis swishes water around in his mouth, spits it out. "When I boy of ten, no rain fall on Brava. Crops shrivel. Thousands lie down in road and die. My father, he sail trading ship to Africa. Say he bring food. But he never come back."

Luis shakes his head, like bad memories is crawling through his hair.

"Week after week, I watch for ship. Mama's bones poke from her skin. Hair fall out. She scream while fever burn her brain. When she breathe her last, I wrap her in strips. Dig grave myself. Watch for next whaler coming into bay, swim out to it. Cap'n Jordan take me on as cabin boy."

"Our Cap'n?" I ask, surprised.

But Luis don't answer. By now he's staring at the sea like he's a child again, hoping to see his daddy's ship. And a moan is coming from somewhere in his deepest self.

Seem to me Luis is fixing to have a fit, same as a mad dog I seen one time in Edenton. It howl for hours before it die, like it's crying over all the sorrows of the world. That's Luis, all right. I reckon his mind got twisted when he was young. He seen too much too soon.

Long about then, Cap'n shows up. He talks quiet to Luis, like he done this many times before.

That's when it comes to me, Owen. We sailors is

all different colors. All of us—you, me, Isaac, Luis, maybe even the English fellas—we all got different stories. But some time or other, every last man of us is from the same place—the Land of Misery.

Joseph

---

*10 June 1847*

Dear Owen,

Last month the *Ivy Ann* pass the Friendly Islands and the Marquesas. Last week, we recross the equator. Cap'n says Honolulu in the Sandwich Islands will come into sight soon. You can tell from the pictures why he sends grog to the fo'c'sle most every night.

I can't ever drink all the rum, cause it burn my throat. So Luis pluck it from my hand, finish it for me. Luis does like his ration of drink.

Joseph

*6 August 1848*

Dear Owen,

We been circling this wide Pacific for almost a year. Filled a thousand barrels so far, but the whaling is off and on. Betweentimes, boredom is like the plague. When one of us catches it, the others get it too. Then fists fly over simple things, like somebody cheating at checkers, or who can carve the best picture on a whale tooth.

Every month or so, another whaler sails into view. Then Cap'n lets us row over and have a party with them sailors. Seeing new faces and hearing fresh news keeps our spirits up.

Today we speak to the *Jupiter*, a whaler that dock last April at the Sandwich Islands. While in port, the sailors hear that somebody discover gold in California. It was just a-laying in the American River next to Mr. John Sutter's lumber mill. Fistfuls of gold, them sailors say, enough to fill the crown of a hat!

When the *Jupiter* put in at San Francisco last month, five crewmen jump ship. They head up to the river, sure they will strike it rich.

I'd jump too, if I had the chance. Food on the *Ivy Ann* is filthy as ever. If we lucky, we catch a porpoise, and Cook makes stew. It tastes as rich and sweet as shad. But no fruit means we all got bloody gums and achy bones.

The bad food brings up whispers of mutiny. When Luis hears it, he swears he'll kill anybody who touches Cap'n. Turns out this is Luis's sixth whaling trip with Jordan. I guess cap'n is his only family, and the *Ivy Ann* his only home. He don't want to lose either one.

Lately I been dreaming of Edenton. Gran is in her rocker, and Lulu is playing with a muslin dolly. But Mama don't come to me in dreams, maybe cause I have not freed her yet.

Joseph

OFF THE COAST OF CHILE
*12 November 1848*

Dear Owen,

The weather is turn cool and wet. All the crew is wearing oilcloth suits to keep the rain off. We have fill thirteen hundred barrels with oil. Cap'n says we is homeward bound!

The fishy sailors been talking about ships breaking up around Cape Horn. A few is vowing to never touch grog again. Others is on their knees at night, praying. This worries me some.

Joseph

CAPE HORN
*27 February 1849*

Dear Owen,

We been sailing south by east for three weeks, squeezing through the Cape straits. The mountains on either side is covered with a mantle of snow. Look dreary, like old men huddled under blankets.

Storms come up every day. Some is rough enough to rip the mainsails off the poles. We replace them with spare sails, but we only got two left. Lose them all, the *Ivy Ann* tips over and sinks. Then I join you on the bottom of the sea, Owen. Only I won't have no canvas shroud between me and the sharks.

I now make this promise to you. If ever we get around Cape Horn, I am reading the Bible from start to end. I am never running again without saying good-bye to my family. I am never lying again long as I live. If I live.

Joseph

BERMUDA
*22 April 1849*

Dear Owen,

Can't tell if I am living, cause the *Ivy Ann* is anchored off a place that seems like heaven. Bermuda is a smallish island fringed with pinky sand. There's plenty of whales beyond the sandbanks—enough to fill the rest of the barrels so we can head home.

I have cut two maps from Uncle John's geography book and figured out our route. This is been a heap of work, I don't mind saying. But it gives me something to do in that quiet time after sunset. Besides, I want you to see where all we been.

The right line on this first map shows the beginning of the trip, before . . . before you leave us. The left line shows our homeward trip from the Pacific to the Atlantic.

And the second map shows where we been in the years between.

One week, Owen. Then I commence to set Mama, Lulu, and me free.

Your friend,
Joseph

# Part IV

## New Bedford

1849–1851

# Owen

*2 May 1849*

Dear Owen,

Home! When we slip into New Bedford harbor, Cap'n orders us to raise all the ship's flags. They is waving proud in the breeze as we hove to.

Wives and children on the dock wave back, happy as birthday cakes, shouting hurrah at their menfolk. The sight make me hungry for my own family, till I spy a familiar face. It's Moses Shepherd, the fella who owns the rooming house where I stay three years ago.

After the sailors tie up, I strut down the plank with the donkey on my shoulder. Step onto the wharf, but the ground is rolling under me.

"Halloo, Mr. Shepherd," I call, laughing at myself. "Looky, I got the legs of a jellyfish!"

He don't hardly say hello back before he takes hold of my wrist. Marches me up Elm Street to his boardinghouse. I glance over my shoulder, see Luis heading with Isaac and the others to a tavern. Think I might just turn around and join them, till I remember what Luis is like when he drunk.

I keep walking, though Shepherd surely means to give me the what-all. "You never told me you had family in Boston," says he. "Or that you left them without a fare-thee-well. Your uncle was looking for you."

"Uncle John! Is he still here?"

"He first come in late fall of forty-six. Said he was searching for a short boy, sixteen years of age. Said maybe this young fella had a thirst for a whaling adventure.

"I tell him I remember you," Shepherd goes on, "and your gambling habits as well. I tell him you and the *Ivy Ann* is long gone."

Then Shepherd tells me that John come back this past March. Says that he and Mama is moved to Rochester, New York. Lulu is boarding at a school about a hundred miles from there. Uncle John write down the mailing address. He ask Shepherd to make sure I get it when the *Ivy Ann* return.

I got to stop now. I'm writing Mama a real letter and mailing it tonight. Telling her that before two weeks is up, I be living with her in Rochester. I won't write about the freedom money, though.

The news will knock the hat right off her head, and I can't miss that. It will be the proudest one minute of my life.

Joseph

---

*3 May 1849*

Dear Owen,

The crew lines up in front of Mr. Chase's office at the docks this afternoon. We get paid, all right, but my share is only $217.96.

That's not all. Chase subtracts $75 for the clothes and supplies he give me before the trip. Takes $50 for my share of the rotten food. Another $35 for paying dockhands to unload barrels from the *Ivy Ann*. My haul for three years of blood and boredom is a grand total of $57.96.

When Chase hands me the money, my spit turns vinegary. "Is this a rich man's arithmetic?" I ask.

He crosses his arms like he Mr. King of the World. "Jacobs, you signed a paper agreeing to a lay of 1/188. Extra charges were explained in the paper, too."

About then, the sound of gravel grates in my ear.

"Greenies don't get much. Colored greenies even less."

When I turn around, Luis is behind me, sweating worse than a horse been rode all night. "You looking awful green yourself," I reply. "You swill too much grog yesterday?"

"When whaler come home," he answers, "sailor men drink. Sailor babies run off."

"Shut up, Luis," I say.

Then Isaac comes along, pay in hand. The two of us walk up the hill. "Luis is right about pay for colored sailors," he say. "Right about greenies, too. You'll get more next voyage."

I pull a face. "You got enough to buy that farm now?" I ask.

"I surely do," he answers, a yellow gleam in his eye. "But why waste time on farm fields? It's goldfields and pay dirt I'm after now. I'm off to California. Going to find me a pot of gold!"

A pot of gold! My mouth drop open. "I wish you luck, then."

Isaac shakes my hand. "Good-bye to you, Joseph. Remember what I said about passing. Think it through first."

Then he disappear around the corner. Three years of knowing somebody, and in one second, it's like they never live at all.

I stomp up the hill to the rooming house.

Study Uncle John's arithmetic book again, check Chase's figures. The subtraction is right, but I don't know how much Chase get all told for the oil. So I can't know if he pay me 1/188 of the total profit.

Even if he has, I see now that the bigger the number on bottom, the less I get. And 1/188 of anything is nearly nothing at all!

I got to write Mama again. Tell her I'm moving to New York for a job that makes real money. She can visit if she want. Only one thing I feel all right about. Mama won't miss her freedom surprise, cause she didn't know she was getting one.

Joseph

---

NEW YORK
*23 May 1849*

Dear Owen,

Mama and I meet in New York City at a house on Fourth Street. The man she used to work for buy it when he get him a new wife name of Cornelia Grinnell. Miz Cornelia take me to Mama in the parlor, then leave us alone.

I hand Mama a bunch of violets I buy on the street. She smother me with thank-yous and kisses, and we sink into a pair of fancy stuffed chairs.

When Mama ask about whaling, I tell her only the good parts—watching stars, dancing jigs, talking to you and Isaac.

"What's this John tells me about your gambling?" she ask.

"Oh, it's nothing, Mama. Them days is long over."

"I'm glad to hear it. Gambling is a sign of weakness, not like you at all."

"What about Gran?" I ask. "You hear from her?"

"Now and again she gets someone to write letters for her. She sends them to me in care of a free sailor. Gran always says to tell you to be a good boy."

I smile, cause Gran will never think of me as a man.

"She tells me I should not neglect you," Mama say, her voice cracking. "But that's what I did, Joseph. I left you to suffer at the hands of those apprentices."

"That's over too," I say. "What about folks back home? Gran ever mention old Dave Blount or Josiah Collins? Or a sweet girl name of Comfort?"

"No," Mama reply, "though I did learn that James Tredwell died, and his wife, Mary, moved to North Carolina."

"So you done the right thing!" I say. "Sure as the

world, Mary would have taken Lulu with her, and Sister be a slave in a slave state!"

Then I take a deep breath, cause it hurts to speak of Samuel Sawyer, especially to Mama. "I got to ask about my daddy. Does Gran ever see him? He ever give her Lulu's and my free papers?"

"No," Mama answers. "He moved to Norfolk, Virginia."

Her eyes film over, and she does not seem to be in present time. "The terrible years under Gran's roof . . . the pain . . . and my children are still not free."

She plucks at the violets, rips the petals off one by one. "Gran says Norcom still brags around town that you and Louisa belong to his daughter."

"Why won't they leave us alone?" I cry.

"Norcom has always craved power over me," Mama says in a dead tone. "Now his grown daughter craves money. I am thirty-six, still of childbearing age and worth a thousand dollars on the auction block. More children means more property, you see."

"More property," I repeat, while the horror of what Mama is saying breaks over me. "Children who would be my half brothers and sisters. Children to sell or work to death."

Mama nod. "After returning from England in forty-six, I moved to Boston. Somehow Matilda Norcom discovered my address there. She sent a letter that increased my fears tenfold. I must come back to Edenton, she wrote, or purchase myself. John suggested I move to Rochester to be with him."

Purchase herself. What I would give to help Mama do just that!

Then Mama rambles on about how relieved she is to be in Rochester. That the many abolitionists there will protect her from Matilda Norcom. And she's helping John run an Anti-Slavery Reading Room where people pay to read books and pamphlets. It's in the same building as Mr. Frederick Douglass's newspaper, the *North Star*.

But I only half listen, cause I'm thinking about Matilda. Now that she's stepped into her daddy's shoes, she can go before an Edenton judge herself. If Matilda comes after Mama, she won't waste the trip. She'll want Sister and me, too. If only I had the money to pay her off!

Owen, *why* didn't I read them sign-up papers for the whaler? You might think I'm hating the Norcoms tonight. You wrong. I'm too busy hating myself.

Joseph

NEW BEDFORD
*2 June 1849*

Dear Owen,

Mama and I agree that New Bedford is the best place for me now. I can earn a living here, and Matilda Norcom is got to know it's a haven for runaways. She would get no help from police here.

So I'm boarding with Moses Shepherd again. Hauling barrels in the day and slipping into old habits at night. I wouldn't tell Mama for anything, but I been playing whist again. Losing, too. I've sailed over most every ocean that God put on the earth, Owen, yet it seems like I haven't moved an inch.

Joseph

---

*3 February 1850*

Dear Owen,

John's reading room never has make any money. When he close it last fall, Mama leave Rochester. It's risky, but she need an income. So she's back in New York, working for Miz Cornelia and taking care of her new baby girl. Poor Mama. Too bad she don't have a dollar for every mile she's traveled trying to make a safe home for herself. She could be buying her freedom by now.

I been thinking of other ways to get our freedom money. You suppose Isaac ever find him that pot of gold?

Joseph

---

*16 June 1850*

Dear Owen,

Last week I write my uncle, ask him what he thinks of the gold rush. He writes back that the *North Star* reprint an article by a white Southerner living in California. This man reports that digging for gold is so hard, only three kinds of men is cut out for it: the Negro, the Indian, and the Irish.

I guess we is more like each other than we thought, Owen! If you was here, we could have us a long hoo-ha over that. Then we could go to

California together, prove the Southern man is right.

But Mr. Douglass writes in his paper that armed bands of slaveholders is moving to that state, bringing their slaves with them. John don't want me to go. Says it's a sure sign of danger for all coloreds there. He's plenty anxious about a new federal law in the making too—the Fugitive Slave Act, it's called.

Owen, your mama ever give you a sugar-water rag to suck on when you a baby? This new law is like that. It satisfies slavery people, cause it overrules free-state laws that protect runaways now.

Here's the details, best as I understand them. Even if a master isn't chasing a runaway, people got to turn in a colored that they know is a fugitive. If somebody like Matilda Norcom *is* chasing a fugitive, bystanders on the street got to join in the hunt. Otherwise, they is breaking the law. Anybody who refuses to help, the judge slaps a thousand-dollar fine on him, puts him in jail.

The Fugitive Slave Act sews everything up nice and neat for slaveholders. There is one tiny hole, though. If the slave run while in a free state, the law don't apply. My uncle remind me he escape from Sawyer in New York, so he's in no danger. It's Mama and me and Lulu who keep him awake at night, cause we leave out of North Carolina.

If the act passes, John writes, ex-slaves in the

so-called free states should arm themselves. He says the lives of coloreds will never be the same.

Ask me, they can't get any worse.

Joseph

---

*20 September 1850*

Dear Owen,

Oh, these is awful times! President Fillmore sign the Fugitive Slave Act two days ago. My family is easy pickings, now more than ever.

Suppose Matilda Norcom flaps her eyelashes at an Edenton judge. She comes north with a paper saying she owns Mama, and what Mama looks like. Matilda shows the paper to a federal marshal in New York. He captures Mama, locks her in jail.

Then Mama stands in front of a New York judge. If he finds her guilty of being a runaway, he gets ten dollars. That's a sweet deal for him, isn't it? Next, Matilda forces Mama back to Edenton. Might sell her to the first slave trader who comes to town. Mama be gone from us forever!

Matilda might bring another signed paper too.

One proving she still owns Lulu and me. Mama and John think Lulu is completely safe at her school, and even with the new law, they pretty sure that whites in New Bedford won't let nobody capture me. But they is made a plan, just in case.

John writes that Mr. Douglass is changing his mind about California. He's been getting letters from coloreds out there. They finding two hundred to three hundred dollars in gold every week. So many folks is racing to California that whalers been turned into passenger ships. John is bought a ticket, gone to see the goldfields for himself. If he can stake a claim with a high yield, he'll send gold for my passage, then more for Mama's and Lulu's.

This is not to my liking. I been the one put the gold rush idea in John's head to begin with! But he only has enough money to get himself out there, so I'm staying put. I've decided to use the time for two things. First, studying arithmetic. If I can't be free from white folks, at least I can keep them from cheating me. Second, it's about time I meet some girls.

Joseph

*19 April 1851*

Dear Owen,

Coloreds in New Bedford in a bad way. A runaway name of Thomas Sims been arrested in Boston two weeks ago. Today's paper says his master is taking him back to Savannah, Georgia.

Abolitionists in New Bedford think it will soon happen here, too.

If it does, they say, avoid arrest peaceably. Otherwise, fight to the death! So hundreds of New Bedford coloreds is leaving for Canada. Selling furniture, breaking up families, cause it's easier to travel in small groups or alone.

Lately I can't sleep. The slave hunters find Sims hiding in a boardinghouse for colored sailors. A house just like the one I'm living in. I lie here at night, wonder, did he hear the marshals storm up the stairs? Or did he wake from a peaceful dream, find them looming over his bed? Makes me afraid to shut my eyes.

Joseph

*25 April 1851*

Dear Owen,

Troubles and more troubles. Last week, Mama get an urgent warning from Edenton. Somebody in the Norcom family—Matilda, most likely—is planning to seize her in New York. This makes four times they come north since Mama run from Edenton. With the Fugitive Slave Act backing them up, I guess they figure it's worth the price of another train ticket to find her, maybe me too.

Miz Cornelia Grinnell grow up in New Bedford. She's sent Mama to hide at her father's country house here. It's down an out-of-the-way road, back in the woods.

Mama get a message to me when she first arrive, tell me to meet her at dusk in the gardens back of Grinnell's house. I walk the five miles out there, keep a lookout for policemen the whole way. Find Mama by the rose beds, worn down from running and fear.

I take her arm. "Let's go inside, rest while we talk."

"No, the baby is sleeping," she reply softly, "and we can speak privately outside."

"Baby!" I say. "What baby?" We follow a path away from the house, past a grove of fir trees. They standing straight as soldiers, bristly and mean.

Mama explains that Miz Cornelia insist on

sending her here with the baby girl. Says if the police catch Mama, they have to return the baby to its mother. Then Cornelia could help save Mama somehow.

"Why in the world did she send you to New Bedford?" I ask. "Don't she know we're expecting a pack of slave catchers any day now? I wouldn't trust her if I was you."

"Joseph, you're wrong!" Mama says. "Cornelia hates slavery! She could go to jail for helping me. How many mothers would let their child travel with a fugitive? This has put her babe in danger too."

"That's what I mean. It seems *too* good of her."

Mama looks at me with sad doe eyes. "Joseph, you can't lose trust in all people. Save a little for the ones who deserve it.

"Terror reigns in New York," she goes on. "It's crawling with slave catchers. Since the law passed, I never leave Cornelia's house without wearing a veiled hat, and I always ride in a carriage. For the time being, New Bedford is safer. Matilda can't track me down in this secluded spot, but she could find you in town. That's my greatest concern now. We've got to get you out of here."

"Have you heard from John?" I ask.

"Not a word, nor a dollar's worth of gold. If only Samuel had given you those free papers so long ago!"

*If, if,* I think. If the slaveholder do this or do that. *If* is all my life comes down to. I bring up something been on my mind since the Sims mess.

"Mama, I'm thinking I should leave the colored boardinghouse. Move to a white one and try to pass for white. There must be twenty thousand whites in New Bedford. It be easy to blend in, long as I stay on their side of town."

"Yes, anything to keep the marshals from finding you," she says, but the way her shoulders cave in, I can tell something more is on her mind.

"Don't worry, Mama. Just look at me. After the winter months, I'm pale as cream. You wear a veiled hat to hide your face in New York. I can wear my old whaling cap to hide my hair here. Wear it on the streets, at the docks, sleep in it if I have to!"

She puts her hand on my head.

"Such sweet curls," she murmurs. "Pretty as a halo. But, I worry that the cap won't be enough. Matilda would remember your face well enough to describe it to the police. And I worry . . . I worry that if you cross over to the white world, you might never come back to me. I would never see you again."

"Are you telling me not to do it?" I ask.

Mama smile a little, but her eyes fill up. "I suspect you are too old for telling, son. You must make up your own mind. If I don't see you next Sunday, I'll know your decision."

I snap off a rosebud, roll it in my hand. Find

myself wishing you was here, Owen. You'd help me get the ticket money somehow, just like you get the money to leave Ireland. We could hop on a passenger ship, be gone by sunset tomorrow.

The wail of the baby stops my wishing. Mama kisses me like it might be the last time, then scurries back to the house and her half life as a runaway. And I walk the five miles back to mine, try to decide what to do.

Joseph

---

*25 May 1851*

Dear Owen,

I have not turn into a white man, after all. I decide that Mama right. Matilda see me most every day while I was growing up, and them Norcoms got long memories. When I show up that next Sunday, Mama relieved, say I got too much spirit to be white. Thinks I'd get myself in trouble, give myself away.

Last week Miz Cornelia send Mama a letter with a false return address. She write that Matilda must have give up and gone back to Edenton, cause they haven't seen her. So Mama is gone back to New York

City with the baby. She try to convince me she be safe there, but we both know better. I don't know who to worry about more, Mama or me, cause no place is safe.

With Mama gone, the summer is passing slow as mud. Meeting girls isn't easy. I seen plenty of young ladies on the streets, but they always with strict-looking mamas. I even went to church one time, thinking I'd meet somebody. That preacher talk so long, he give me a headache. I sneak out after two hours, leaving him still praising the Lord!

And card games no help, cause I have give them up for good. Every cent I earn on the docks goes in my donkey. I can't wait for John's gold. I got to get my own self to California.

Joseph

---

NEW YORK
*28 December 1851*

Dear Owen,

I'm writing from a colored boardinghouse in New York, but I won't be here long. Am leaving tomorrow on a passenger ship. I plan to stop by Miz Cornelia's house this evening, tell Mama good-bye. I been putting it off, cause Mama don't know my plans yet, and her tears generally make my heart low.

Joseph

---

*29 December 1851*

Dear Owen,

Good news for once! Mama glad to see me, but even more excited about a letter she just get from John, written months ago.

I follow Mama to the parlor while she talks a red streak. "He's moved downriver to Negro Shallows," she say, "near a place called Mormon Island. He's with a crew of five men, and they've gone so far under the hill that they work by candlelight. People are finding gold, he writes, where they never thought of looking for it. He says it's given new life to mining."

Mama plop in a chair, breathless. "His letter with gold should arrive soon. Then you can leave."

"Mama," I start off, "I'm leaving sooner than you think." Then I tell her my plans, and she takes it well.

Tears up some but agrees. "Yes, you best go. Thankfully, the Fugitive Slave Act doesn't apply in California. You won't be tempted to pass. . . ."

I lose patience with her. "Why shouldn't I pass? I didn't ask to be born a slave! Didn't ask for a white daddy, either, but as long as I got his light skin, why not use it?"

Mama slip her hands in mine and squeeze. "Because one day you might regret giving up who you are—a colored man with a colored family who loves you. It is not a simple matter of wearing a hat. It stands for a lie that blots your family from your life. We might soon be out of your heart as well. Promise me, Joseph. Promise you won't do it unless it's necessary."

So I promise, Owen, cause I can't tell her no in the middle of saying good-bye. I give her a hug at the door. "It near kills me to leave you behind," I say.

Mama draws herself up tall as a tiny woman can. "The Fugitive Slave Act gives us no choice," she replies. "Just remember. Leaving doesn't mean we stop loving each other."

*Neither does passing*, I almost shoot back. But for once I am wise, swallow the words.

Joseph

# Part V

## California

1852

# Mama

San Francisco
*3 May 1852*

Dear Mama,

By God, I have kept my promise to you. Kept it though I had to live four months in steerage, near the bottom of the ship. That's where they stuffed the colored passengers. Steerage is worse than a fo'c'sle on a whaler, Mama. Sailors spend most of the day on deck. Steerage passengers are only allowed a few hours up in the light. I guess white people own the sun, along with everything else in this country.

Now and again I found a place to sit on a bench, but most times I hunkered on the plank floor. Slept there every night, too, except when we went around the Horn. Nobody slept much during those three stormy weeks.

So I been a man of my word, though I've paid a price for it. At least the long months at sea gave me a chance to study John's books and work some on my grammar. But I believe it's time to reconsider my promise.

The ship docked in San Francisco Bay around dusk. The minute I stepped off, I bought a paper and read the news. It happened in April, while I was at sea. California has passed its own Fugitive Slave Act!

Mama, I feel like a cat in a drawstring bag. Laws keep pulling those cords tighter and tighter. You know the story. The slaveholder sends a slave hunter out here. When he finds the man, he takes him before a judge, claims he's a fugitive. Just like back East, the judge can return the runaway to slavery.

I'm not safe in this state, after all. Matilda Norcom wants me bad enough, she'll put a sharp-eyed slave catcher on my trail. Without free papers, I won't stand a chance in front of a California judge.

I always thought I'd get back to Edenton sometime. Keep my promise to Gran that I'd see her again. But not like this, not at the end of a chain.

Joseph

*4 May 1852*

Dear Mama,

After four months of steerage, I decided to sleep last night under the stars. This morning I wandered through town. San Francisco is a wild place! Rickety wood buildings sprawl every whichaway across the hills. Thousands of men swarm the crookedy streets, eyeballs wide with the thought of gold. Most are white, but there's Mexicans, too, skin warm as copper, and Chinamen the color of butterscotch.

These men made me wonder just what the word *colored* means to white people. Then I spied big letters scrawled on a sign in a store window: NO COLOREDS ALLOWED! I figured this was good a place as any to start living a white life.

I slip on my old whaling cap and step inside. Nod at the white man behind the counter. "A floppy-brim hat, please," I ask real calm, but my hands is aquiver. "A map, blanket, and packet of beef jerky, too."

He takes his slow time getting them from the shelves. I don't want him seeing my trembly fingers, so I put the money on the counter while his back is turned. Then he wraps everything nice and neat in paper, gives me the package. "Thank you," he says, all chipper. "Good luck at the digs!"

Mama, you wrong about me not handling myself.

It's easy to fool white folks! I grin and stroll to the door, but then I notice a ruckus in the street. The storekeeper looks over my shoulder. "What's going on?" he asks.

At first I see only a dust cloud and a crowd of people. When they back up, I catch sight of a colored man pounding the tar out of a white one. Somebody pulls him off, and the white man flips the colored to the ground. Smashes him with a stick, screams, "You're my slave! Refuse to go with me, and I'll give you two hundred lashes!"

Well, he's beating that slave so hard, the bystanders cry, "Shame!"

Long about then, I spy another colored man standing off from the crowd. He has a pick in one hand, something like a pie pan in the other, and a stripe of scars on the side of his head. It's Isaac, my sailor friend from the whaler days. A fine man, Mama, a strong one, but he doesn't help that slave. Neither do I.

Isaac glances up, and his eyes catch mine. He takes it all in—my cap, the window sign, the white man behind me. My friend turns his back to watch the fracas another minute. When the crowd makes way for the police, he disappears faster than smoke.

"Slave or free, they're too much trouble," the storekeeper grumbles. "If it was up to me, none of them would cross the state line."

I don't stand around to argue. *Maybe I should find Isaac,* I think, but my legs hurry me in the other direction, till I see a white hotel. I stand in front of that wide double door, wonder if I should chance it.

A young colored bootblack is working off to the side. While he polishes the white men's shoes, they talk like they own him. That decides it for me. When a group of colored men pass by, I follow them to the colored section. I see a hotel there, enter as myself.

It felt peculiar, Mama. Like I was a spirit, floating through walls. San Francisco has a post office, and I could mail this letter easy enough. But then you'd know the truth of what your son did today.

Your son,
Joseph

---

EAST OF SACRAMENTO
*10 May 1852*

Dear Mama,

A boat trip from San Francisco up to Sacramento costs thirty dollars. That's more than I got, so I set out walking. It's been hard going. Thousands of wagon wheels and men's feet have made ruts deep enough to snap an ankle.

I've tramped all day toward the snow-topped Sierras in the distance. It's a good thing I'm only going as far as the high foothills, as I'm running out of food. I built a fire to keep me company, but the night sky on a prairie goes on forever, Mama. It feels big enough to suck me up, if howling coyotes don't get me first.

Joseph

MORMON ISLAND
*13 May 1852*

Dear Mama,

My feet have nearly give out. I been walking north for three days. Reached Mormon Island early this morning. You never saw such confusion. Thousands of miners are strewn across the hills, or standing in the river, or passed out from too much liquor. Every kind of hardworking, sober, staggering drunk man you can imagine, and all filthy. Portuguese, Chinese, Mexican, Irish, Germans, South Americans, and a few Indians, too. I figured I didn't need my hat—that these fellows were too lit up with gold fever to care about one short colored man from North Carolina.

This town got one street that runs alongside the river. Most everybody lives in tents on either side, but a few have built cabins. There's some signs of civilization—a bathhouse, saloon, supply store, and barbershop, though most men don't seem to care what they look like.

And I don't know why they would. You'd think from California that God never made daughters, mothers, sisters, or wives. Since reaching this state, I've seen exactly two women, and they were saloon ladies in Frisco.

I walked around, learning the different ways a man can find gold. Some miners stand in the cold water, dip pans with holes in the bottom into the riverbed. They bring up gravel and shake it through, hoping gold is left behind. Others run sluice boxes on the banks of the river. A sluice box is like a horse trough with holes in the bottom, same as a pan. Gold mining looks easy. Seems to me all a man needs are a few tools and a fondness for mud.

Then I came upon something that iced my heart—a white man with two colored men helping him dig straight down into the ground. The way he gave them orders made me think he was a Southern slaveholder.

He glanced my way once, then looked again. That did it, Mama. I put on my floppy hat and won't ever take it off, not in this town. Most miners wear them all the time, anyhow.

After that I quick found me a privy. Sat in there a long while, cause my stomach was hurting bad. Passing won't be as easy as I thought. Truth is, when white men look at my face, I'll never know what they see.

I'm heading out now for Negro Shallows, if my feet will let me.

Joseph

---

NEGRO SHALLOWS

Dear Mama,

After a six-mile walk, I finally reached Negro Shallows. Nothing much here. Twenty tents or so, and a few shanties. I found John sitting on the bank of the river, chewing a hunk of hard bread.

"Joseph, Joseph," he cries, leaping up, "you've come at last!" I throw down my pack, and we talk a while. I tell him what's been happening in New Bedford. He tells me about the colored abolitionists he met in San Francisco before coming up here.

We hash over the California Fugitive Slave Act too. John seems low about it and everything else. I believe his body and spirit are broken, Mama. His hands are swollen from too many hours with a pickax, and his eyes got a dull look. Same one that sailors get after months of lean eating and spoiled water. After the talking winds down, I lay back, think I'll rest up from my trip, but John's got other plans.

"I can allow one hour of rest," he says, kind of snarly. "Then your work begins."

I draw a cup of water from the pail, but John snaps, "No gulping. It costs fifty cents an inch."

I lean over, peek into a pot of fatty stew on the campfire. "If you're hungry," says John, "use my plate."

"What are them gray pieces of meat floating in the pot?" I ask.

"Day-old squirrel." John tosses a pickax my way. "Don't be long," he says.

With that, he turns his back and trudges across the shallow stream. I watch him disappear inside the hole that he and his team have dug in the hill.

Uncle John is determined as an ant, Mama, carrying a load of worry too big for one man.

Joseph

FREEDOM SHALLOWS
*12 June 1852*

Dear Mama,

The name of this camp troubles me. I have renamed it Freedom Shallows to suit myself. I know a new name doesn't change anything, but it cheers me anyway. And I need that, cause my hands are bleeding from days inside that hard mountain.

The hole only goes back a few yards, so I can still see daylight. But nighttime, I can't make out much by the candles. I never do see the streak of gold that John swears is just behind the ore.

Yesterday a miner on our team told me about the gold rush in Australia. Says he heard that all a fellow needs is a hundred dollars for a ticket to Sydney, and enough to buy a digging license when he gets there.

"Yessirree," the miner said. "Gold everywhere, blinking in the sun."

This has started me thinking, cause gold mining in California is pitiful, just pitiful. The rock yields about an ounce of grains every day—little more than a thimbleful. At sixteen dollars an ounce, it barely pays for water we buy here in camp, or the tools and food that John buys in Mormon Island. Once a week, Uncle wraps our gold dust in a handkerchief and heads for the Chinamen's tent store there. He comes back with supplies, then another useless round of digging begins.

Most men here are in the same fix. That's why they live for their weekly dance. Today is Saturday, so they'll get likkered up some this afternoon. Tonight a couple of fellows will play fiddle and banjo while the rest do-si-do with each other. John told me he has no time for such nonsense. "You go to the dance," he says at breakfast. "I've got to leave early in the morning for supplies."

"Uncle," I say, "I'm in no mood for banjo music. Never will be. Anyway, who wants to dance with a man? You go. Let me fetch the supplies tomorrow."

John wrinkles his lips. "Very well, but avoid the gambling tents. Cards will rot a man's soul."

"You take care of your soul," I spit back. "I'll take care of mine."

It's time I start standing up to John.

Joseph

---

*Sunday—13 June 1852*

Dear Mama,

A lucky day at Mormon Island. I was asking for coffee and jerky at the tent store when I overheard two white men talking. They were boasting about winning at poker in the gambling tent next over.

I left without my goods, slipped into the tent. It was smoky in there, packed with miners sitting on boxes around tables. I stood behind a game, watched a while. Figured I was safe from my card-playing self, cause I know nothing about poker.

But Mama, it's easy! I know you don't approve of the game. Maybe that's cause you don't understand it. Players ante up a little money for the pot, see. After the dealer gives each player five cards, the betting begins. When that's done, the draw starts. You can trade up to three bad cards for new ones. If a player wants to drop out of the game, he folds.

One more round of betting, and you lay your cards down. If you holding two of the same cards, you only got a pair. That's not much. A flush—like five hearts or five diamonds—is real good.

A full house is two of the same and three of the same, like two eights and three jacks. You holding that, you flying to the sun. Whoever holds the best hand wins everything in the pot. Simple!

Only hard thing is keeping what you feel inside. That way, nobody can guess if you holding good cards or not. It's called a poker face.

After I watched a few games, a husky, blond-headed man turned around. Said his name was Stuffy.

"Pull up a box," he says real cheerful. "Join us!"

Before long, I've bet John's gold dust and won it back, along with two dollars. I play another round, win another three. You know what, Mama? Whist been the wrong game for your boy all along. I'm meant for poker!

When I leave, Stuffy tells me the big jackpot games are late at night. He says men bet fistfuls of money, bags of gold dust, even nuggets. Who knows? Maybe one day I can buy our freedom, after all.

Joseph

---

*Sunday night—1 August 1852*

Dear Mama,

I've gone back to the gambling tent every Sunday. Wear my floppy hat each time, win most times too. One week I lost almost everything, but now I got a hundred dollars hid in my pack.

John's been going to the dances every week. I believe the merriment has done him good. He's been laying off work at sunset, not talking so rough. But all that changed tonight. Tonight we roasted a chunk of pork I bought at Mormon Island today. I had to rob a few dollars from my savings, but I liked watching Uncle lick his fingers, enjoy himself for a change.

After supper, he stretched out, stared at the growing moon. It was cool white, the shape of an egg. A few tents away, the fiddler was playing some high, homesick notes to keep himself company.

"Joseph," says John, "you must have paid a good deal for the pork. I marvel that you had enough left over for other provisions."

"Oh," I lie, "the Chinaman had one extra roast. He sold it cheap."

"We'll feast on beefsteak," John promises, "as soon as we hit a vein."

"Uncle, ever think of going to Australia?" I ask. "Maybe we'd do better there."

John pushes himself to his elbows, surprise in his eyes. "Mining is discouraging, I'll grant you that. I'd rather be in San Francisco, working with abolitionists. But let's not forget your mother and Lulu. We must find enough gold for their passage here."

I throw what's left of my coffee on the fire. "That's just what I'm saying! We can buy steamer tickets in Frisco, go to Sydney where the real gold is."

"We have no extra cash," John says. The words

sound disappointed, like the look that's always on his face.

"Leave it to me," I say. "I have resources."

"Resources," John repeats. I can tell he's considering possibilities in his mind.

"The truth, now," he commands. "Is it something unsavory? You have not turned to thievery, have you?"

"Uncle," I reply, "I always did obey my elders. Gran and Mark. You and Mama. Simmonds in the print shop, Cap'n on the ship, Moses Shepherd. I'm twenty-two now. I've had enough bosses. Let me handle myself."

John stands and draws his arm back. It was a hurtful thing to watch in the moonlight—my onliest uncle raising a fist to his onliest nephew.

"Tell me," he threatens.

I grip his arm till he lowers it. "Uncle," I beg, "go to sleep. I'll see you in the morning."

But he won't see me in the morning, Mama. I can't work alongside John anymore. I got to strike it rich my own way.

Your son,
Joseph

*2 August 1852*

Dear Mama,

Soon as the first lark sang, I rolled over, made sure John was still asleep. Put some jerky in my pack, checked to see I had the money, a tin of matches, and a bit of fishing gear. Before daybreak I was gone from Freedom Shallows.

After reaching Mormon Island, I wandered around till dark. Played a few warm-up hands, then joined Stuffy's late-night game. Besides him, two other players were at the table.

Left of Stuffy sat a sour-faced farmer from Ohio. He was wearing overalls and puffing a stubby cigar.

Right of Sour Face was a red-eyed miner with a satchel and a gin jar. Looked like he'd been drinking all day. I can say for sure he needed a two-dollar bath awful bad.

I sat on Red Eye's right, trying not to breathe through my nose. One figure was solid in my mind. Ship tickets cost two hundred dollars. I had one hundred, needed one hundred more.

While Stuffy shuffled the deck, Red Eye pulled a drink from his jar. He got to cursing the Chinamen who run the tent store.

"Coolies!" he roars. "Them Chinee ain't

Americans. Got no right to be in Mormon Island. Mexicans, too—lazy greasers!"

"It's the digger Injuns that bother me," Stuffy adds, cutting the cards. "Rooting around for grasshoppers and such to eat."

Mama, the only Indians I've seen been digging for gold, same as white miners. But it's true that the Chinamen are a funny-looking sight. They wear baggy clothes and long pigtails down their backs. Still, they polite as any men I've ever met, and their store is spotless. That's refreshing in a mining camp.

And near as I can tell, Mexicans are the smartest miners here. They dig up ore from the riverbank and grind it between heavy rocks, like millers grinding corn. Mexicans find as much gold as anybody else.

But I hold my tongue. Decide too much rides on this night to get in an argument.

"Coolies and greasers," Sour Face snorts, gnawing the cigar. "Waste of time. I'm after negroes. Them runaways bring a high price."

Without thinking, my hand flies to my head, touches the hat. I feel a strong urge to visit a privy, but Stuffy is already setting the game and the rules. "Five-Card Draw," he announces. "Five dollar ante. Can't bet no higher than what's in the pot."

Stuffy, Sour Face, and I put in our money. Red Eye roots through his pockets. He fishes out five dollars for the ante and almost falls off the chair.

Stuffy deals us each five cards. I get a pair of queens, a nine, a six, and a two. A pair of queens, Mama! Only need one more for three of a kind.

The betting begins. Sour Face glances at his cards, throws five dollars on the table.

"I'll see your five and raise ten," I say.

Red Eye fumbles through his satchel. "Out of cash," he mutters. "But I got this."

He tosses a nugget big as an apple on the table, then slumps forward, chin on chest. Stuffy whistles, and every man in the tent wanders over to gawk. The lump appears to weigh around fifty ounces. It's worth at least five hundred dollars and likely much more.

Stuffy yanks Red Eye by the hair, lifts his head a few inches. "You heard the rules!" he hollers. "You can call with the nugget, but forty is the most it's worth in this game! You calling?"

Red Eye nods. Stuffy lets go and matches his forty. Right about then, Red Eye lurches from the chair, staggers to the tent flap, and heaves up the gin. The men honk with laughter, tickled by this fool and his lost fortune.

With Red Eye out of the game, I know my chances are getting good. Until I hear the drunk's slurry voice say, "No coloreds 'llowed!"

I look up, see Uncle John stepping over Red Eye. He peers through the gloom. "Is Joseph Jacobs here?" he asks.

Sour Face swivels around, stares at me. "This your man?"

My man. He means my slave, Mama.

"Oh, yes," I answer clearly. "He's mine."

"Go on, John," I call. "I'll meet you back at our tent directly." John leaves without a word, his face stiff as death.

After the betting ends, the draw begins. Sour Face stands pat, keeps all his cards.

"Give me two," I say, hoping I sound regular. Like ordering a slave around is something I been born to. I pitch my throwaways, the six and two, on a pile. Sour Face grins a bit. He knows the best I can have is three of a kind, and he's holding something better.

Stuffy deals me two new cards. When I lift the tops, I see a nine and a lady wearing a crown. *Steady now,* I tell myself. Lean back like I got all the time in the world.

Stuffy trades in one card. The bet's to me. I put down fifty-five dollars—every cent I got. Stuffy looks at his card and folds, disgusted. It's to Sour Face.

Sour Face calls the fifty-five. We lock eyes. I can tell he's wondering what my high bet means. He falters, lets his bet stand with no raise. The round is over. "What you holding?" he asks, flipping cigar ashes on my boot.

Slowly I fan out a pair of nines and three queens—a full house! Sour Face yanks the cigar from his mouth, slings down a flush of five clubs. He stomps out of the tent with thunder on his face.

A few of the men slap me on the back, and I let myself smile. *Oh, glory,* I'm thinking, *it's mine, mine!*

But I've lost my uncle in the getting of it.

Joseph

---

*4 August 1852*

Dear Mama,

Hard as I try I can't make myself face John. After the card game, I found a spot under an oak tree and slept till dawn. When I woke up it was already hot—a dry, baking heat that stole the spit from my mouth.

I headed for Freedom Shallows. Walked along the ridge trail for a while, but decided the river route might be cooler. So I slid down the bank and followed a side stream into a stand of piney woods.

That was two lonesome days ago. I been camped here ever since. Sometimes I take out the money and count it. Or I bounce the nugget in my palm, weigh its heaviness against the heaviness of my heart.

This is a sweet place, Mama. The stream is shallow and only ten feet wide, but there's silver trout in it.

Plenty of deadwood for fires is lying around too. Beyond the pines is a scallop of round-top hills, and a platter of sky so blue, makes me ache for an Edenton spring. Maybe I'll stay here forever. Might as well. Got nowhere else to go.

Joseph

---

*5 August 1852*

Dear Mama,

I've learned one thing. Being alone too long can wreck a person's mind. Nighttime falls, tree limbs turn into long crooked arms. The *hoo hoo hoo* of an owl sounds like the chuckling of a ghost. Funny thing is, by dawn everything seems regular again. That's why I paid no mind when I heard a loud sound this morning. *Rustle, thud. Rustle, thud, plop.*

Wasn't till I was on my knees, hunting through my pack for matches, that the noise got in my head and froze me up. John has told me time and again to take care in these hills, cause this is mountain lion territory. When I spun around, I knew my time on earth was about spent.

Instead, I saw an Indian girl at the end of the

grove, on the other side of the stream. She looked to be a few years younger than me, with rich brown walnut skin. Pretty skin, Mama. Real pretty!

She wore a straw skirt, a deerskin shirt, and a necklace of husks around her neck. And she had the longest, thickest, shiniest pile of black hair I ever laid eyes on. I stood quiet, watched while she leaped up to a pine bough and beat it with a stick. When pinecones flopped to the ground, she tossed them in a basket.

To tell the truth, I didn't know what to do next. These last three days, I've only talked to you, Mama. Sometimes I almost think I can hear you talking back, but it's not the same as a real voice. I needed that bad.

So I make my way through the woods and down the stream. "Hallo!" I shout, edging closer. "My . . . name . . . is . . . Joe-suf!"

By this time, only the rippling water is between us. She looks at me without a sign of fear. "Joe-suf," she parrots. "My name Mulka."

"Let me help you with them pinecones!"

She shakes her head, and that ties my tongue. I find one last hunk of jerky in my pocket and offer it to her. Turns out this is the best thing to do. Mulka steps across boulders in the stream, light as a bird, and grabs the salty beef.

It's clear the girl is hungry, but she sniffs the meat and hands it back. Says, "Cow meat not the people's food."

"It's some people's food," I reply.

"Only one people," she insists. "Nisenan. It mean the people. My people."

This was the beginning of a mixed-up conversation. Mulka told me her family claims the land nearabouts but doesn't own it. Nobody owns it, she said. I never figured out what that meant, but I did learn she's got a mama, daddy, two brothers. Their true home is a village near Sutter's Mill, where gold first turned up.

Then she says mining has ruined the hunting grounds and streams down there. Her people eat pinenuts, dig for grasshoppers and roots, and make acorn bread, same as always. But it's not enough, so the Indians are starving. That's why her family moved to the high foothills. They can still find a few deer and elk up here. It's easy to get lost in Mulka's eyes while she tells me all this, cause they're soft and pretty. Real pretty.

Seemed to me like food was the best way to please her, so I offer to catch and cook us some breakfast trout. She hangs back a bit, but I guess she's been lonesome too, away from her village and all. She nods yes, and I go get my fishing gear. We sit quiet on the bank while I strip a branch for a pole. I keep my eyes to myself, try not to stare at her. "This is a fine spot," I say, tying a worm to the hook. "No miners yet to dirty it up."

"It my special place," she agrees. "Water clean. Gathering good here."

After I catch two trout, I make a fire, roast the fish in the ashes. Mulka smiles as she eats, but when I ask how she knows English, the smile falls off her face.

"My grandfather," she answers. "He dig gold for John Sutter at his mill. Learn English from Sutter, teach my family. One day, white miners come to mill. They shoot Indian miners. Grandfather live two days. Then his heart go away to place in sky."

Mulka sighs, stands. She takes off her necklace, hands it to me. "You give me gift of meal," she says. "I give you gift too."

She turns to go. "Don't leave!" I cry. "I can climb the pine trees, shake branches you can't reach."

"No," she says firmly. "My father not like it if he find out. He say white men no good."

"White," I gasp, laughing, cause I'm not even wearing my hat. "I'm not white, Mulka!"

Her eyes are full of mistrust as she looks me over. "You lie, Jos-suf!" she shouts.

Bare feet flying, she hauls off through the woods and back across the stream. Snatches her basket, runs toward the hills. "Wait, wait!" I call, till the words fall into the hollow space she's left behind.

And I'm sorry. Sorry for the hunger and killing, but mostly sorry for myself. Mama, this is a cruel joke. First girl I meet in years, and she spurns me for being white. I pick up the necklace, put it in my pack. Find a twig and scratch words in the parched clay.

pretty little negro    chinee    milk-and-molasses
coolie    injun    mick    portugee    digger
greaser    high yellow    brown joe

The hateful words stare up at me, till I stub the toe of my boot in each one. Rub hard as they go back into the earth, where they belong.

Never again am I letting other people decide who I am. Never, and I got a necklace to remind me of it. Breaking up camp now. John and I got some talking to do.

Joseph

---

*Noon*

Dear Mama,

Something wrong when I reach Freedom Shallows. I went inside the mountain, but the miners said they hadn't seen Uncle all day. I hurried down the packed paths between every tent in camp. No sign of John.

So I'm writing this letter to think things through. Mama, can you hear me begging over the mountains and the miles? I'm going up into the high hills now. Pray, please pray, that I don't find John's limp body hanging from a lion's mouth.

Joseph

---

*Midnight*

Dear Mama,

What a time, what a time! I hunted all day, came back at dusk without John. Decided to sleep a few hours, then set out again with a torch.

But when I open the tent flap, I hear, "It's over, Joseph."

I crawl into the tent and find John in a huddle under his blanket. "Uncle, is this where you've been all day?"

"You're not the only one who can disappear."

"You've got every reason to hate me. Just let me explain. . . ."

John rolls away and buries his head in his arms. "They sold her. Sold her like a bushel of squash or a peck of corn."

"Sold who?"

"The day you left, I went to Mormon Island looking for you. I stopped by the post office." John shoves a letter at me.

"It's dated last March. Took five months to reach us. I wanted to tell you, but I had no idea where you were. Then I passed the gambling tent. I have thought all along that you would answer the call of the cards one day."

I look away. Sometimes John knows me better than I know myself.

"Open the letter," he says.

Mama, I still can't believe what happened. How you were reading the newspaper, saw Matilda and her husband listed as guests at a New York hotel. Or that you ran from New York to New Bedford again, till Miz Cornelia raised three hundred dollars to pay for your freedom. And Norcom is dead at the age of seventy-three, leaving his family in debt! No wonder Matilda took what she could get for you.

"John," I cry when I finish reading. "Why are we holed up in this tent? We should call the fiddler. Hold a dance, sing and shout. Mama don't have to run anymore!"

But John is still in some deep pit in his mind. "How can I celebrate in this no-soul country? Where Harriet is purchased as property in a free city? Where my own nephew must deny me?"

John breaks down then, Mama, and it is the sorriest thing I've ever seen. I try pulling him up, but he won't budge. I crawl out of the tent, grab his boots, and yank. Finally I get him sitting up proper outside. "Uncle, I know I hurt you," I say, "but I did it for us."

Then I show him the nugget. "We can leave California! Start over where color don't matter!"

John stares at the gold. "Is there such a place?"

"Maybe not," I admit. "We've got to see for ourselves."

"I should stay here," he mumbles, rubbing his forehead. "Offer my skills to antislavery forces in San Francisco."

I notice stale coffee sitting in the pot, so I build a fire and heat it up. Give John a few minutes to fight the war he's having with himself. "What if you want to be white again?" he says when I hand him the cup.

"I won't ever! Passing reminds me of standing in a crow's nest. The fear makes me sick, cause I never know when somebody will find me out. Besides, being white can jump back on you, bite you hard. You ever have a lady friend, Uncle?"

"Once, back in Edenton," he answers, puzzled. "That was years ago. I've forgotten all about her—had to. Why do you ask?"

"No reason," I answer, cause I won't tell him about Mulka if he can't remember how it feels to like a girl.

"One thing, Joseph," he says. "If we go, you must give up gambling. It's low class." John's mouth takes on that wrinkly look.

I cut him cold. "Uncle, Australia is kind of a gamble, anyway. Ship could sink, or folks might not take kindly to coloreds when we get there. We got to have faith. I bet you five dollars I won't be gambling in Australia. Cause we will fill our pockets with gold!"

Your son,
Joseph

---

*15 August 1852*

Dear Mama,

My head is full of many things. We're staying at the colored hotel in Frisco and leaving early in the morning. Most fellows here are going to Australia on the same ship. The dining room was crowded with them tonight.

We found two seats at a long table, joined a group of chattering miners. Some talked about meeting women in Australia, most talked about finding gold. One fellow, a blacksmith by the look of his fingernails, worried that slave catchers would follow fugitives to Australia.

"The country belongs to Great Britain," John explains to him. "United States laws don't apply."

"I'm relieved to hear it," the blacksmith says. "After what I seen yesterday, I ain't never coming back to this country."

He grabs a saltshaker with one calloused hand. "A Southerner come out here for gold. He seen his runaway slave in a camp down by the Tuolumne River. Good luck for the white man, bad for the slave. Soon as the slave spot his massa's face, he take off and run to Frisco.

"But the white man hurry here too. He go before a judge and get a warrant. The police stop the slave while he running by my shop. Put a ball and chain on him right in front of me. The massa tow him toward Long Wharf. They headed back east, by ship, I guess."

I was glad to see the old spark light up John's eyes. "Do you know the runaway's name?" he asks. "There are abolitionists right here in San Francisco. I'll speak to them this very night. They can organize a protest!"

"No name," the blacksmith replies, his mouth full. "But he got white scars on the left side of his head. So deep, the hairs don't grow there. Hard to miss."

Oh, Mama, Mama! Once I step foot in Australia, I'm free as a song. While Isaac has gone back to Virginia, his feet chained and one ankle dragging a thirty-pound lead ball. After all these years, the more we coloreds run from slavery, the faster it catches up.

Joseph

16 August 1852

*Dear Mama,*

*A real letter to my free mother! I've got to write fast and mail it before we board the ship.*

*I tossed all night with one thought in my mind: laws, and how they've had us on the run for so long. In twenty minutes John and I are leaving for a place so far away that American laws can't ever rule us again. Mama, I don't want them ruling you and Lulu, either.*

*I bet you're surprised to find a bank note for five hundred dollars in this letter. Here's what I want you to do with it. Write Matilda Norcom. Offer her money in exchange for Lulu's emancipation papers. Then Sister can be free once and for all.*

*Mind you, John is dead against us paying for Lulu. He says Sawyer already paid Matilda's daddy years ago, and we shouldn't give the slaveholding witch another penny.*

*I tell him that one thing is plain as grits. Sawyer won't ever care that his own children are still slaves by law. No sense trying to get free papers from him. We got to get to the root of the thing.*

*That means Matilda. Maybe she's so broke she'll take whatever low amount you offer, Mama, but at least you'll have negotiating money. Spend it all on Lulu if you need to.*

*Whatever you do, don't try and pay Matilda for me. No piece of paper can ever make me free, cause in my head, I already am. I'm nobody's slave, nobody's high yellow or milk-and-molasses man. From now on, it doesn't matter what people call me, or what they see when they look at my face, or what I see when I look back.*

*When Sister is finished with school, the two of you can come to Australia together. Maybe you can talk Gran into coming too. Tell her that yesterday her boy seen a shiny shawl in a store window. Made in India, with silver threads sewn on gold cloth. I bought it for her, but she's got to come get it. Then we'll all be together again, and I can keep my promise to her at last.*

*On that bright day—when our family is far from this slaveholding, color-crazy land—we'll be finally, truly free.*

*Your son,*
*Joseph*

1852–1860

# Joseph

## The Rest of His Story

As the character of Joseph sails off into the west, we can turn now to the real Joseph Jacobs. He probably left for the Australia gold rush sometime in 1852, and he probably knew that Dr. James Norcom was dead. What he didn't know was that Norcom had played a vicious trick on the Jacobs family years before.

When Norcom sold Joseph and Lulu to a slave trader in 1835, he had indeed committed an illegal act. By law, the children and their mother belonged to his underage daughter, Matilda. But two years later Norcom repaid Matilda. He gave her two enslaved children in exchange for Joseph and Lulu.

The bill of sale is dated 1837. It states: "I, James Norcom . . . in consideration of the sum of five hundred dollars received from the sale of two mulattoe Slaves named Joe & Louisa, the Children of woman Harriet, do grant . . . unto Matilda Norcom two negro slaves, the children of Melah named Penelope and John."

The substitution meant that the original sale was final.

Unfortunately, no one in the Jacobs family ever learned of it. Joseph and Lulu were more free than they knew.

It would be nice to think that when Joseph and John went to Australia, they found a place where color didn't matter. For many, it didn't. The Australia gold rush was even more international than the one in California. It drew adventuresome gold diggers from around the world. These men were of every color and class.

A Polish miner named Seweryn Korzelinski described the mix in his memoir: "A colonel pulls up earth for a sailor; a lawyer wields not a pen but a spade; a priest lends a match to a Negro's pipe; a doctor rests on the same heap of earth with a Chinaman; a man of letters carries a bag of earth; many a baron or count has a drink with a Hindu, and all of them hirsute [hairy], dusty and muddy, so that their own mothers would not recognise them."

But sadly, color did matter to the native people of Australia. Aboriginals there were displaced by gold mining, just as the Nisenan Indians were in California.

It would also be nice to think that Joseph and John found gold. The truth is, we know only fragments of what happened to them. These tantalizing clues are in letters that mention their letters.

Joseph and John Jacobs probably arrived early in 1853. Four to six months later—about the time it took a letter from Australia to reach the United States—John wrote to a friend in Boston. He told the friend that he and Joseph were proceeding to the mines.

But Harriet had no word from them. "It makes my heart sad to tell you," she wrote to a friend in October 1853, "that I have not heard from my brother and Joseph."

While Harriet waited, she looked to spiritualism for comfort. Spiritualists believed that during a séance, a medium could contact the spirit world and speak to the living or dead.

A medium must have told Harriet that Joseph and John were alive. The anxious mother rejoiced when she received a letter in the summer of 1855. John and Joseph were mining in Parramatta, a gold-rush camp near Sydney.

It was "just as the spirits told me it would be," she wrote to a friend, "even the very Language was in the letter. . . . I was so happy to know that they were living."

Another letter arrived from John in 1856. We don't know what it said. He may have told Harriet that he was planning to give up gold mining, because in 1857, he wrote again. This time he mailed the letter from England, where he was working as a seaman.

Joseph remained in Australia and wrote for a while. Then the letters stopped. Worried, Harriet wrote and begged him to give up digging and come home.

In 1860 Harriet finally received another letter from Australia. Written by a stranger, it asked her to send four hundred dollars in gold so Joseph could come home. The writer of the letter explained that Joseph had been suffering from rheumatic fever for some time. He could barely hold a pen.

Rheumatic fever is an inflammatory disease caused by

an infection. It can affect the skin, brain, heart, and joints. Joseph's supposed symptoms matched the illness, but we don't know if he really had rheumatic fever.

The letter writer asked Harriet to mail the money to Melbourne, a gold-rush city south of Sydney. Harriet sent gold by a trusted lawyer, and it arrived safely.

The following year, the Civil War broke out in America. It lasted from 1861 to 1865. While Harriet watched the country rip itself to pieces over slavery, she also watched for Joseph. Perhaps she thought he was waiting for the conflict to end before coming home.

But even after the war was over, Joseph failed to arrive. The letter asking for gold was probably a fraud.

In November 1866 Harriet asked a fellow abolitionist, Lydia Maria Child, for help. Joseph's trail ends with Child's letter to a minister friend in Australia. In the letter, she encouraged him to ask other ministers to announce from their pulpits that a young man was missing. His mother, she wrote, "was in great distress about him."

If the ministers read such an announcement, it never led to finding Joseph. As far as we know, he was never heard from again. Maybe one day another long-forgotten letter will turn up and give us a clue about his fate in Australia. Until then, the mystery remains unsolved.

# An Author's Expedition

## PUZZLES

As an author and abolitionist, Harriet Jacobs is equal in importance to the more famous Frederick Douglass. Her son's life deserves close attention. If you're interested in my thoughts on the real Joseph Jacobs, read on. If you're reading this book for a book report, you can stop here if you like.

In 1861, shortly before the Civil War, Harriet Jacobs published *Incidents in the Life of a Slave Girl*. In the narrative, Harriet described her years in Edenton and Boston. To make her story more accessible for young people, I wrote a historical novel, *Letters from a Slave Girl: The Story of Harriet Jacobs* (New York: Scribner, 1992). Since then, I've spoken with thousands of young readers about Harriet Jacobs. Someone in the audience usually asks, "What ever happened to her son, Joseph?"

I've long wanted to write a book that could answer this question, if only in part. For a while, I considered writing Joseph's biography. I rejected the idea for two reasons. First, every biographer needs quotations—words spoken by the subject of the book. In *Incidents in the Life of a Slave Girl*, Harriet recalls Joseph's speech only five times. These few one-way snippets of conversation weren't enough for a biography.

I had another problem with Harriet's memory of her son's words. Most of Joseph's sentences sound wooden. On arriving in Boston, did the twelve-year-old from rural North Carolina really say, "O, mother! How d'you do?" or "I bid her good-bye"? As a North Carolinian myself, the words rang false.

Though events in *Incidents* actually happened, Harriet invented dialogue when she wrote the book. To create speech for various characters, she used Southern dialect, Irish dialect, or standard English. Sometimes she changed the dialect for the same character. I had no way to know if Joseph's five quotations represented his real voice.

Second, a biographer needs facts. I didn't have enough. It's true that Harriet often mentioned her "light-hearted" son in *Incidents,* but only as part of her own story.

We know of just four events in Joseph's life after he left Edenton: his abuse at the hands of Irish-American boys in Boston; the three-year whaling journey, because, as Harriet wrote, he was "too spirited a boy" to suffer further in the print shop; and the trips to the goldfields of California and Australia.

The skeletal facts made me wonder. After Joseph went North, how did he handle the pressure of Norcom's repeated hunts for his mother? The danger of living without free papers? We know Harriet's version of Joseph's feelings—recalled years later—but parents don't always get it right.

I also wondered about Harriet's attitude toward the Irish. In her narrative, she writes about them four times. The longest passage describes Irish coachmen who crowded around her at a train station in New York. One of them tried to cheat her.

Harriet wrote, "I inquired whether his conveyance was decent."

"'Yes, it's dacent it is, Marm,'" the Irishman answered in a dialect that Harriet used to re-create his words. "'Devil a bit would I be after takin' ladies in a cab that was not dacent.'"

But it wasn't decent. Harriet's desperate escape was finally coming to an end. It's no wonder that the loud Irishmen made her feel "half-crazed," as she wrote in *Incidents*. To be cheated by one of them must have seemed like the last straw.

And any mother would be furious to learn that other boys had abused her son. The incidents with the coachman and the apprentices in the print shop left Harriet with angry feelings. Like the settled white people of Boston, she may have decided that the Irish were an inferior race. Even Irish people born in America were not quite American citizens to Harriet. The boys in the print shop were "Americans," she wrote, "or American-born Irish."

But did Joseph feel the same way? Thousands of homeless Irish immigrants poured into the North End of Boston while he lived there. He would have seen them begging on every corner of the neighborhood.

Could Joseph identify with their hunger if he had never

been hungry himself? With their homelessness if he had never been homeless? Likewise, could an Irish boy understand what it felt like to be hunted by slave catchers? We know that while John Jacobs was in Boston, he gave money to an Irish famine relief fund. Did John's sympathy influence Joseph? These complicated questions intrigued me.

I also wondered how Joseph passed for white when he worked at the print shop. It was probably accidental, because he must have assumed that people in Boston were like those in Edenton. In slaveholding America, especially the South, a person was legally white *or* black. There was no in-between, no white *and* black. But what if later he deliberately decided to pass? Would his family have understood the necessity, or would they have felt betrayed?

Finally, I wondered if the real Joseph's ideas about race changed. He surely met men of many colors on the whaling ship and in the goldfields. How would a boy from black-or-white Edenton deal with the rainbow of skin tones? Would he have noticed the plight of California Indians?

No one can answer these questions factually, but that doesn't stop us from imagining. This is the task of any historical novelist: to imagine the life—voice, thoughts, and deepest heart—of someone who lived in the faraway past. And so, with many puzzle pieces to sort through, I decided to write a work of fiction about the "light-hearted" and "spirited" Joseph Jacobs.

## DECISIONS

When writing historical fiction, I start with everything that I or others (usually scholars) think is true. To create my fictional character of Joseph, I looked closely at important dates in the real Joseph's life.

In *Letters from a Slave Girl*, I used a birth year that scholars agreed on: 1829. After rereading *Incidents*, I realized there was another possible date. Harriet writes that Joseph was twelve when she fled north by ship in June 1842. Joseph, I concluded, might have been born in 1830.

Some researchers believe that Joseph left for California with his uncle in 1850, and that later they mined for gold on Muiron Island, off the west coast of Australia. After reading a letter that Harriet wrote in early 1852, I discovered two interesting details. First, she mentions seeing Joseph often in 1851, when John was already in California. So Joseph and John didn't go to California together. Second, she wrote *Mormon* Island, not Muiron Island, in her slanty, hard-to-read script.

Shortly after the gold rush began in 1848, people of the Mormon religion dug for gold on a gravel bar in the American River. Their settlement became known as Mormon Island. It was a thriving tent city during the gold rush days. Several African-American camps were within a few miles of Mormon Island (the entire area is now under the waters of an artificial lake). My guess was that John lived in one of these camps. Which one? I had no way of knowing, so I created the fictional Negro Shallows.

In *Incidents*, Joseph arrives in Boston and announces, "I can read, and she [Lulu] can't." I wondered who taught Joseph to read. His great-grandmother, Molly, and his great-uncle, Mark, were illiterate. It's possible that Harriet taught Joseph before she went into hiding, but he was only five. This would be early for most children. If Harriet taught Joseph to read, she never mentioned it in *Incidents*.

And who could have taught Joseph to write? Josiah Collins IV seemed to be a good candidate. He and Joseph were the same age. During some of the spring and summer months, they lived only three blocks from each other. Many slave narratives and white slaveholders' diaries describe interracial childhood friendships. The friendship I created in *Letters from a Slave Boy* is completely fictional, but it was certainly possible.

As with *Letters from a Slave Girl*, I decided that letters in *Letters from a Slave Boy* wouldn't be mailed. In real life, it would have been dangerous to mail letters to Edenton, New York, and Boston. The text or postmarks might have given away Harriet's location (though letters passed along the underground maritime railroad were safer).

Whaling crews wrote letters with little hope that passing ships could deliver mail to its destination. So most sailors kept journals, as the fictional Joseph does in his diarylike letters.

My character of Joseph could have mailed letters when he

was in San Francisco. He also could have mailed them from Mormon Island, which opened a post office the year before he arrived. But would he want his mother to know that he sometimes passed for white? Or that he was gambling again? When I asked him, he answered with a definite no!

I based Joseph's misspellings and word usage on examples from his mother's and Uncle John's writings. As slaves, neither Harriet nor John could attend school. Their spelling was often phonetic (*prisan* for *prison*), and their grammar was typical of uneducated North Carolinans, both white and black, at the time. Throughout their lives, Harriet and John continued to teach themselves standard English. I decided they would have urged Joseph to do the same, and that his grammar and spelling would improve somewhat, just as theirs did.

The character of Luis speaks pidgin, or contact English. This simplified vocabulary and grammar makes it easy for speakers to communicate when their native languages are different. Luis's native language would have been Kriolu, a mix of Portuguese and West African words. Kriolu is now the national language of the Cape Verde Islands.

I based sentence construction for the voice of Mulka on interviews with Nisenan speakers in *Ethnology of the Nisenan* by Ralph Beals (Berkeley, California: University of California Press, 1933).

The Smith School of Boston, Massachusetts, was built in 1835. The first school constructed in the United States for African-American children, it is now part of the New England Museum of Afro-American History. *Courtesy of the author*

William Simmonds, the Boston printer who probably apprenticed Joseph Jacobs in 1845. Apprentices were bound by law to serve a full seven-year apprenticeship, but by 1845, the law was no longer enforced. *"Jerry, with memoir" by Walter Aimwell [William Simmonds], 1864.*

No. 489 District of New-Bedford, July 27 1846

Age, 17
Height, 5
Complexion,
Hair, black
Eyes, black

I Joseph Jacobs do hereby certify that was born at Edenton in the State of NC according to the best of my knowledge and belief.

David H. Chase

Protection paper issued to Joseph Jacobs, New Bedford, Massachusetts, July 27, 1846. After escaping slavery, African-American sailors often forged or exchanged protection papers to hide their real identities. *Courtesy of the New Bedford Public Library, New Bedford, Massachusetts*

Boys on whaler "trying" blubber, or boiling whale flesh to render oil. *© The New Bedford Whaling Museum*

A boatsteerer from the whaler *The Wanderer* aims his harpoon in this 1923 photograph. *© The New Bedford Whaling Museum*

San Francisco, 1850. Ships arrived at and departed from Long Wharf, as seen in the center of the painting. *Courtesy of the California History Room, California State Library, Sacramento, California*

An African-American miner shovels earth into a sluice box at Auburn Ravine, 1852. Auburn was a gold-mining camp about twenty miles north of Mormon Island, California. *Courtesy of the California History Room, California State Library, Sacramento, California*

A miner named Hiram Dwight Pierce reached Mormon Island on the South Fork of the American River in 1849. Pierce wrote in his journal, "The scenery at the river is wild to the extreme." *Courtesy of the California History Room, California State Library, Sacramento, California*

## NINETEENTH-CENTURY RACIAL SLURS

Racial slurs and terms in this book are taken from actual nineteenth-century letters, narratives, and newspaper articles. None are acceptable today. I have included a glossary so that readers can better understand the language that the character of Joseph heard as he traveled the world.

**Chinaman:** Chinese man.

**Chinee:** *Chinese* in pidgin (or contact English).

**Coolie:** *day laborer* in the Hindi language of India. Used in gold-rush California to refer to Chinese immigrants.

**Digger:** insulting term for Irishmen. In California, *digger* also referred to Nisenan Indians.

**Greaser:** insulting term for Mexicans or Indians.

**High yellow:** insulting term for light-skinned African Americans.

**Mick:** insulting term for Irishmen. Also *mike.* Both short for Michael, a common name in Ireland.

**Mulatto:** originally a Spanish term for a person of any mixed ancestry. In America, a person of white and African-American ancestry.

**Negro:** *black* in the Spanish and Portuguese languages. Most nineteenth-century African Americans preferred *colored.* Eventually they accepted *Negro* but insisted on capitalization.

**Portugee:** *Portuguese* in pidgin (or contact English).

## Suggested Reading

**If you're curious about the Irish famine, whaling, or the California gold rush, try the following titles written for young readers:**

Lyons, Mary E., ed. *Feed the Children First: Irish Memories of the Great Hunger.* New York: Atheneum, 2001.

McKissack, Patricia and Frederick. *Black Hands, White Souls: The Story of African-American Whalers.* New York: Scholastic, 1999.

Murphy, Jim. *Gone A-Whaling: The Lure of the Sea and the Hunt for the Great Whale.* New York: Clarion, 1997.

Stanley, Jerry. *Hurry Freedom: African Americans in Gold Rush California.* New York: Crown Publishers, 2000.

**If you want to learn more about nineteenth-century race relations, try these more challenging books written for adults:**

Grover, Kathryn. *The Fugitive's Gibraltar: Escaping Slaves and Abolitionism in New Bedford, Massachusetts.* Amherst: University of Massachusetts Press, 2001.

Handlin, Oscar. *Boston's Immigrants: A Study in Acculturation.* New York: Atheneum, 1968.

Lapp, Rudolph M. *Blacks in Gold Rush California.* New Haven: Yale University Press, 1995.

Starr, Kevin and Richard J. Orsi, eds. *Rooted in Barbarous Soil: People, Culture and Community in Gold Rush California.* Berkeley: University of California Press, 2000.

# Acknowledgments

A thank-you to my Irish friends, Myra and Niall Horgan, for their assistance with Owen's dialogue. Thanks also to Lauren F. Winner for her wise suggestions, and to Ann J. Lane, who long ago pointed out the special difficulties of escape for enslaved mothers with very young children.

Thanks also to Jean Yellin, who has devoted many years to the study of Harriet Jacobs. I hope that *Letters from a Slave Girl* and *Letters from a Slave Boy* create a new generation of readers for her edition of *Incidents in the Life of a Slave Girl.*

Most of all, I thank Joseph Shea-Hackett, who brought a young reader's perspective—the most important kind—to my story of Joseph Jacobs.